SMOKE
ON THE
MOUNTAIN

SMOKE ON THE MOUNTAIN

by

Ellen Crain

DODD, MEAD & COMPANY

New York

Library of Congress Catalog Card Number: 67-13366

Printed in the United States of America
by Vail-Ballou Press, Inc., Binghamton, N. Y.

To
Richard K. Abbott

Although the background for this story is historical, the action taking place in the Great Smoky Mountains during the time land was being acquired for the national park, the characters, events and incidents are entirely imaginary. The story was written in sympathy for the old natives, descendants of early pioneers who carved from this beautiful and rugged wilderness a way of life so distinctly individualistic, their story cannot be ignored in our American heritage.

ELLEN CRAIN

SMOKE
ON THE
MOUNTAIN

I

GRANDMA WELLER seldom talked of the past any more. No one else was left who could share these remembering years with her. If sometimes she reached back into her memory searching for comfort, if at these times her eyes were dreamy and vague, folks said Grandma was getting queer and was not responsible.

Grandma never heard these conclusions voiced in words but she saw the eyes that expressed them and, for each pair, she had a pity kindled with humor and understanding. She had a feeling of charity that dispensed in services of healing the very knowledge her years had given to her, and which the recipients of her healing powers took now without pay or recompense.

Her ninety years sat heavily upon her shoulders and bowed her back to meet a cane that she had carved from a hickory sapling. The hand that clutched the support was a hard and callused claw—long, twisted fingers that were never still. The skin was stretched over the bones of her face like brown rubber, its elasticity spent in rivulets of flesh that crossed and intermingled, hanging in wasted and left-over ends under her chin. Earth-worn and sky-weathered was Grandma, part and parcel of the wind, sun, and rain.

When her husband Ethan died and left her alone at the age of seventy, she had accepted her lot without complaint or regard that her situation was pathetic. To Grandma, independence to do for one's self was exceeded in value only by the pride that prompted self-sufficiency. She had worked and filled her needs alone for over twenty years and she had been too busy with her affairs and those of her neighbors to be affected by the transition about to take place in the mountains. Moving the people to the valley had been like the cry of "Wolf! Wolf!" It was idle gossip and unsubstantiated rumor. This for all the cry had worked great changes in her neighbors' attitude and ways of living. There was a growing feeling of impermanence everywhere.

There was no longer a unity of feeling. Each was a family in itself and each man seemed bent upon his personal aims and intent. Not a fragment was left of the old spirit of survival handed down from early settlers. This old spirit had accepted defeat in nothing, not even death. For where the parent tree fell before the axe, its seed flourished and carried on, blood for one's blood, loyalty without question, recompense without reason. Share and share alike was the old cry of the wilderness and out of this had grown a community interest, a neighborliness that made of this tiny cove a kingdom in itself, each family leaning and depending on the other and held together by the wise dictum of an old granny woman whose words were law even as her healing powers were divine. But not any more.

Grandma Weller sat in the doorway of her cabin one morning smoking her pipe, using the last of her tobacco. She pulled her shawl a bit more tightly around her shoulders and moved so the sun would strike her back. Grandma was worried over that pain in her shoulder. It was a funny thing she could brew medicines and tonics to cure everybody on the mountain excepting herself.

She cocked her ear when a low rumble, growing louder and clearer, sent the hound dog Ezra whining under the steps.

"Autymobeels." She sniffed. "It's getting so a person ain't got no privacy a-tall."

When the car stopped, Ezra grumbled low in his throat. A man sat in the car, his eyes taking in the rising sweep of land back of the cabin, the ridge beyond where the timber stood tall and massive. Then his gaze came back to the cabin, to the crone hunched in her hickory rocker. He opened the car door and walked up the path.

"Hello, Granny," he called.

"I ain't your granny, feller."

The man laughed. "They told me you would be like this," he said.

"Who?" she demanded.

"Why, the people round and about. They are mostly friendly, you know. My wife heard you had a little sugar chest and I came by to see if we could trade."

"Huh!" Grandma sniffed. "Trade, eh? Well, I ain't seen

3

nothing you summer folks has got I'd want in the first place."

Grandma placed her pipe on the floor and, folding her arms under her shawl, she leaned back and began to rock.

"You might as well set down and rest," she invited grudgingly. "I reckon you didn't come just to buy an old sugar chest."

The man smiled as he took a pipe and a tobacco tin from his pocket and seated himself on the step. Soon the smoke drifted in Grandma's direction and she sniffed. Never had tobacco smoke seemed more alluring. She eyed the tin eagerly and when the man slipped it into his pocket carelessly, she sighed with disappointment.

The man looked from Grandma to the cob pipe on the floor.

"I brought you a little present, Grandma, a brand-new pipe and a tin of tobacco. Here, fill it to the brim and see how you like it."

Even as Grandma's eyes caressed the pipe held before her, her body stiffened, her eyes coming to rest finally on the man, in studied suspicion.

"I'm not a land agent, Grandma," the man said, smiling.

"Wouldn't make no difference if you was," she said tartly. "I ain't selling my land. Nobody wants to buy it, anyhow. Nothing but talk, twenty years of talking."

"Well, I don't know about that," the man answered, laying the pipe in Grandma's lap. "Sometimes it takes twenty years to work things out."

Grandma disregarded this remark as not worth considering. It was the same old story and she had heard it too many times. And besides, she was fingering the smooth and polished pipe in her gnarled hands. She looked down and

4

saw the gold band around the bowl, the stem, curved and graceful. Never before had she seen so beautiful a pipe. It cast a spell over her, so that accepting the lighted match from the man was an unconscious movement. The sweet and soothing draft which she now drew into her lungs was strangely satisfying and new.

Along with her well-laid plans, Grandma had mentally filled her bin with a winter's supply of tobacco from Aaron Bigger's crop. Aaron raised the best tobacco on the mountain and was as stingy as a miser, but he'd part with a goodly amount of that tobacco for Grandma. Aaron didn't know it yet, but some of his family would break out in a rash that would keep them awake nights, burning and scratching, moaning and uncomfortable until desperation drove Aaron to Grandma's for some curing salve.

So, even as Grandma puffed on the new pipe in peaceful enjoyment, her eyes closed and her mind moved in reflection.

With the cold snap of Squaw Winter, Grandma had felt for the first time in her life a sort of fear. The pain in her shoulder had kept her wakeful and restless, thinking and uneasy. The firelight flickering on the walls lit up the rafters, empty of onion strings, peppers, sage. Her mind's eye visioned the empty corncrib, the hayless loft, the cellar empty of vegetable roots and other provender. There, too, was the sprinkle of bony chickens, scratching among the clods of last year's garden.

When the cow had wandered off and got lost, when she had viewed the bottom of her lard can one morning and fried the last chunk of salt pork, then Grandma had sat at her kitchen table and viewed her situation with desperate pride and righteous indignation: anger that her years had brought her to such need, that her frailties, which could no longer be ignored, should bend her pride now to public admission of want.

The tears that rolled down her wrinkled cheeks and fell to her twisted fingers was no more than an overflow from a deep well of pride. This pride might admit frustration when alone and in secret, it would run deep and silent, impregnable by the very wall the years had built around it. That well of pride would never be covered with a lid of admission. It would stand open for all the world to recognize and honor, and if it did not gain the recognition it merited, then it would sink deeper and deeper into the soil and bury itself finally with honor. Grandma Weller would starve to death before she would admit either her needs or her inability to meet them.

She opened her eyes now and speculated on the stranger who sat studying her from the porch steps.

"What did you say you come up here for?" she asked.

"Sugar chest," the man answered gently.

Grandma laughed. "Mister," she said, "you are either a good liar or you're the only honest feller I've met from the valley. Now, if a man comes miles to buy a sugar chest, then he knows a value for it I don't know." Grandma took a puff on her pipe, then went on. "I've lived a long time and I've seen surprising things happen. You ain't the only one hunting up old furniture." She leaned forward on her cane and her question was a demand. "What fer?"

The man on the step sat with pipe in hand, studying Grandma. His mission was not so much to please his young wife in search of antiques as to satisfy his curiosity. That Grandma was the oldest resident left in the mountains was

6

point enough in interest. That she continued at her age to ply her trade of midwifery was so astounding to him he felt urged to seek her out.

There lay between this man and the wrinkled old woman before him a great bond of sympathy and understanding. Whether he could, because of his background, overcome a prejudice that lay between them like the mountain peaks rising in the distance; whether he could surmount those peaks and stand on a footing with this wise old woman, he did not know.

As a doctor from the valley, he carried the power of healing to this old midwife, for sick she most assuredly was, whether as a healer she knew it or not.

Grandma sat back in her rocker, dismissing the mission of her visitor as unimportant, this is the face of her personal problems that were so acutely pressing.

"You have a wonderful place here, Grandma. I'd like to think that when my work is done, I could sit and rest in such an atmosphere as this—face those mountains in the distance, hear the creek down there in the hollow, listen to the wind in those trees back on the ridge. There's a sort of company here that makes you feel alone and yet not alone. I suppose you might call it peace."

"I reckon," she answered, "nobody's work is done till their usefulness is gone. You ain't lived long enough yet, mister."

Dr. Mayberry laughed. "I've lived fifty years and worked long enough to look forward to a just rest."

"And when that time comes, you'll know there ain't no such thing as peace. Peace is inside ye, not in and around your house."

"Tell me more, Grandma."

Grandma had met many people from the valley but never one like this man. She looked at him more closely. Yes, he looked all of fifty and there were lines in his face, tired lines. He was tall and rangy like Tom Jenkins. He had a shock of black hair, white at the temples. There was a gentleness about him. Even as she felt herself drawn to him, she wished he would go away now and leave her to think.

He made her think of Callie Jenkins who was always coming to talk things over, and then going away eased in mind. Funny that a person like her could live so long that a second sort of sight came to them. This power however was limited to the folks she knew, to familiar things around her. Grandma closed her eyes, sweeping her visitor from her horizon, going back twenty years and from there to the present.

Twenty years ago it was, since her husband Ethan died. She wanted to kill the mule because the mule killed Ethan, but Tom Jenkins' pa had said she needed the money and Wade Turner gave her fifty dollars for the mule. This with seventy-five dollars that Ethan left was the only money Grandma had had in all these twenty years. It didn't take much money, not with having a cow, and each fall a hog that her neighbors had slaughtered for her. She had her garden and her cornfield. Each spring she hired Tom Jenkins to do her plowing. When the folks needed her in time of sickness or to bring a baby, they came for her in a wagon, and payment for her services was in food-stuffs of various kinds, piled in the wagon on the trip back

8

home. They gave her sacks of shelled corn, potatoes, apples, tins of lard, hams and sides of bacon, buckets of sorghum, and even gallons of corn whiskey. All these things, added to what she herself raised, had kept her in comfort. Her money she spent only for plowing and wood cutting.

She never had been out of coffee, sugar, salt, and spices. Somebody slipped into her house on her trips away and placed these things on her kitchen table. She was sure it was Tom and Sam Acree who contributed these store-bought items but she never mentioned it.

But all this was up to a year ago when the cow got lost and her hog had died. The folks had been so stirred up about the Government buying land, some of them had not even planted crops. Not only that, there had been very few calls for her services.

In the spring, she found the old teakettle empty of money, so she told Tom she didn't feel able to make a garden. She was too prideful to tell him she didn't have the twenty-five cents. Although Grandma did not like leaving home, save on missions of mercy, she had been forced for the past few weeks to visit around a lot in order to get enough to eat. She gathered blackberries and wild plums and canned them without sugar. She borrowed meal from Callie until she could no longer borrow without arousing suspicion. She knew that reproach toward those who failed her now was only an admission of her inability to meet her personal problems. She also knew that she must meet them in whatever way seemed left to her.

So it was that one evening when dusk crept up from the hollow, climbed the hill, and enveloped her cabin in darkness, Grandma fortified herself with her evening pipe and sat on her porch to wait. In two hours now, the moon would be high and full. In two hours, Tom and Callie Jenkins would be asleep, and Tom's field of green corn would be open to her. Just a mile down the road it was, and with the moon clearing a pathway before her, she could go in and borrow just a few ears.

Even as the plan grew in her mind and formulated itself around right and justice, there lay in her heart the grim knowledge that taking what belonged to others was stealing.

Over the ridge, then, came a breeze, light and balmy, sighing through the trees, fanning Grandma's cheek. She thought she heard the wind rustle among the leaves in the new corn. This was the first summer in all her remembering years that she had failed to hear this rustle in her own cornfield; a light rustle, which as summer wore on maturing the corn, drying the fodder on the stalks, and hardening the grain on the ears, grew louder and more pleasurable. The rustle had become to her a promise of plenty, Nature's way of speaking to her.

Soon, it said, I will be ripe for the harvest. Cowpeas growing on my stalks must be gathered and hung to the rafters to dry. Pumpkins hidden among my rows must be placed in the cellar. These are the yield of the cornfield.

All the time the old song was running through Grandma's ears, she was hobbling down the road toward Tom Jenkins' field, reaching out to take the song more clearly to her heart. She did not know her cane hung on the crook of her arm. She didn't know that she walked unaided, driven by a spirit of other years, a spirit that gave her strength she did not normally own. The music of the corn beckoned to her and led her finally inside the rail fence where she stood proudly, listening. Grandma was under a spell of magic that made of the moonlight on the cornfield a mirror reflecting all the other cornfields of all her other years. Each stalk was a human thing that moved and left its shadow on the ground. She did not move into the corn. The corn moved to her and held out to her its fruits, willingly, as many fruits as she could carry.

Only when she reached home and fell wearily to the porch was she conscious of what she had done. She had not meant to do it and yet she had, for there on the floor before her lay two dozen roasting ears, taken from Tom's field, not her own field. She was sick with shame, so she hid the ears behind a barrel in her lean-to, and though she lay in bed for hours, no sleep came to her. She rose from her bed, then, got on her knees and prayed.

"Well, God, what do Ye expect me to do? I can't live on roots and herbs. You send me this worrying heart to punish me, but unless Ye send me something to eat, God, I'll just have to keep on a-stealin' because I don't aim to starve."

She went to sleep, then, and God sent to her a dream. An angel hovered over her bed. As clear as glass she saw him and his words were plain to hear.

"The laborer is worthy of his hire."

To herself she repeated the message and for hours she lay thinking. She had never worked for hire. Labored? Yes. For eighty years Grandma had labored and much of that had been for others, not herself.

Suddenly, she sat up in bed, the tangle unraveled. The

angel had told her she was to be rewarded for her labors. She lay back on her pillows again and as a plan unfolded in her mind, she grew calm and she went to sleep, a smile on her face.

"What are you thinking about, Grandma?"

Grandma came to herself with a jerk that sent a wince of pain across her face. When she clutched her shoulder, the doctor rose quickly and stepped to her side.

"Where is the pain, Granny?" he asked.

She pushed at him with her cane.

"Git away! Git away! Who's talking about pain I'd like to know, and what business is it of yours, anyhow?"

Dr. Mayberry smiled and pulled up a cane chair.

"Funny thing," he said, talking to Ezra, who was stretched at his feet, "a woman will doctor people all over a mountain and for fifty years . . ."

"Seventy!" Grandma interrupted.

"And," he continued, "she expects people to take her medicine and advice but she won't take a doctor's advice when pain comes to her. Funny thing, and foolish, too."

Grandma sat straight in her rocker.

"A doctor," she said. "What ye doing up here, mister?"

"Oh, just a rest and vacation, Grandma. My name's Mayberry, by the way." The doctor stuck out his hand which Grandma merely looked at. Grandma was thinking and she couldn't do two things at once.

"Well, guess I'd better be going," said the doctor, rising. "Grandma, I should think a box of this tobacco and curing you of that pain would be worth a sugar chest."

Dr. Mayberry knew now he was going to come back. He

had been brought on this visit by curiosity and to buy a sugar chest for his wife. The chest was no longer important, and his curiosity had resulted in a deep interest, a desire to help this old woman in more ways than one.

"May bury. That's a pretty good name for a doctor," Grandma said, chuckling.

The doctor turned in the path and walked back to the steps, smiling.

"How about Dr. Weller being a pretty good name, too, Grandma?"

Grandma laughed even harder. The thought had not struck her and she granted the doctor his inning. Suddenly, she realized this man was leaving and she did not know his mission.

"What did you come up here for, anyhow? Old furniture!" Grandma sniffed. "That ain't the reason, and I didn't send for you to do any healing on me. I ain't sick."

Dr. Mayberry set his foot on the step, pushed his hat back on his head, and slouched with his hands in his pockets.

"Do you trust anybody anywhere, Grandma?" he asked.

"Don't trust nobody exceptin' myself," she answered.

"You think you can get along by yourself, live on your pride for food and comforts?"

"I always have up to now," she answered, pridefully.

"What about when all the folks move out of the mountains? The Government has passed a law to make a park of all this land. You think you can get by entirely alone at your age? Some of the folks will be allowed to take money and stay with the land, but the young ones won't do that. They'll all move."

"Yep, that talk's been going around for years, but I

don't put no belief in it. I've got a way of knowing when things is about to happen and nothing has told me this rumor is so."

"It's not a rumor, Grandma, it's a fact. The land belonging to lumber companies has already been bought. The folks living in other coves and on some of the ridges have sold out and moved to the valley. Why, they have bought all the cottages in the settlement a few miles from here. I had to sell mine. We'll be allowed to spend the rest of the summer up here. We can never come back."

A fear went over Grandma and it showed in her face. Dr. Mayberry saw her hand tremble and grasp the arm of the rocker. The Park Commission was moving so fast now, they surely would reach this cove in the next few weeks. This change might come about so quickly Grandma wouldn't have time to arrange for herself. He knew he must come back.

"Grandma," he said, "I must go now but I'd like to visit another time if you'll let me. You say you aren't sick. I've been watching you clutch at your shoulder. There must be pain there, and something causes that, Grandma. I'm a doctor, remember?"

"You mean you got some curin' medicine?" she asked eagerly.

"I've got a whole shelfful of medicines," the doctor answered, smiling to himself.

"Come anytime," she answered, settling back in her rocker and fingering the tobacco tin in her lap.

When the doctor's car disappeared down the road, Grandma sat quietly on her porch, her eyes on the mountains that rose to heights above her cabin. Down in the hollow, Roaring Creek rushed over huge rocks, fell from shelves and ledges in falls, turned with the bends in the hollow. It was music to which she was ever attuned. She remembered what the doctor had said about peace. To him, peace was finding a sameness, something unchanged, and being unchanged it was dependable like the sun rising in the morning and setting at night.

She smiled to herself, knowing that little in life ever remained the same. The mist that hung over the peaks up yonder showed different colors day by day. Some days it hung so low you could not see the mountain tops. The mist spread through the cove in a heavy fog. Fact remained that the mountains did not stay the same and no day was like another day.

He was a strange man, this doctor. Moving to the valley! Grandma sniffed. She didn't believe it. It was the same talk that had been going on for twenty years.

There were six or seven families among her neighbors who were like herself, descendants of the first settlers, their land passed on to them for generations. That they would give up this land and move to the valley was something she could not believe possible. Yet, these neighbors were a great disappointment to her. Yes, life had changed and the old days of helping each other were past. But there was one thing which time and change had not altered and that was herself, her place in this community. She would still retain that place, for the people needed her. There was entirely too much independence of spirit around of late, and she intended to make her folks appreciate her for her worth to them.

She wished now she had asked some questions of that

2

"HEY GRANDMA! Ophie's got something wrong with her. There's a breaking out all over her and she itches something awful. She said for you to send her some of that curin' salve."

Grandma sat forward in her chair, resting her hands on her cane. She had been expecting Aaron Biggers now for several days. Ophie had only to look at poison ivy and it crawled all over her. Grandma also knew this to be the first call on her services since her dream. It wasn't easy to ask pay for helping folks. It didn't come natural to her. It would be breaking a lifetime custom and habit. But, the old custom of having the folks bring things to her had stopped. As for Aaron, he had never given her anything in his life. He was so miserly and so mean that to get out of him what he owed was like taking a cub bear away from its mother. She saw the sacks of cornmeal piled high in Aaron's wagon. He was going to sell it. He would have gone right by her house without a thought of her, save that Ophie needed the salve.

Grandma had only to think of what the whole Biggers clan owed her in years past to draw her to her feet with courage and resolution. Only last year she had safely delivered Aaron's wife, Ophie, of his only son among six children, a son who, so far as Grandma could see and understand, was the only object in his miserly world that received honest attention and affection.

"How is Bertie gettin' along, Aaron?" Grandma asked, in an effort to call Aaron's attention to an unpaid obligation.

"Oh, Bertie is a little pindlin' this summer, Grandma, but it's Ophie I'm stoppin' about." Aaron was in a hurry and he resented this delay. He resented his dependence on Grandma and the airs she gave herself. He stood by his wagon now, studying Grandma, and he felt a change in her. Aaron did not understand. He was merely suspicious.

"Where you taking them sacks of meal, Aaron?" Grandma asked.

"Over to the hotel, Grandma," he answered. "They pay me a good price for this water-ground meal and it helps, too, what with that family of mine. Come on with that salve, Grandma, I'm in a powerful hurry."

Grandma turned and, stepping through her gate, she called back.

"Well, go on and hurry, Aaron. Put a sack of that meal on my porch while I go for the salve."

"What's that?"

Aaron was so astounded he dropped the reins. Gathering

them up again, he faced Grandma, his jaws set and determined, color rising to his hair.

"I said if you're wanting some salve to cure Ophie's breaking out, you could put a sack of that meal on my porch. You think I go around curing people for nothing, Aaron?"

"Well, you have . . ."

"Yes," Grandma interrupted, "I have been a-doing it, and what do I get out of wading in wet leaves, digging and brewing and makin' myself sick? Nothing! Well, I ain't doctorin' folks for nothing no longer, Aaron. A box of curing salve for a sack of meal. Take it or leave it," she snapped.

Grandma hobbled to the house, so full of laughter she could hardly hold herself in. Slipping inside her cabin, she peeped through the door crack. Aaron stood just as she left him, dumfounded and motionless. Suddenly he leaned over, lifted a sack of meal, and fairly threw it to the porch, twenty feet away.

"Aaron," she called. "Bring that meal to the lean-to. Ye think I can lift fifty pounds of anything? Here's your salve and you'd better watch your manners after this if you expect any healing out of me."

Aaron barged down the path, mouthing and grumbling, and Grandma prepared to cook herself some dinner. Her prospects were not very bright.

"You'd think at the end of summer, a person would have all sorts of vegetable roots stored away, to say nothing of jams and fruits."

Taking one of the six remaining potatoes, Grandma cut it up for boiling. With it she added a sprinkle of bacon

19

grease and four balls of moistened meal. She wished she had some turnip greens. Well, if her plans worked out, she would be fixed for eating comforts, come winter.

Leaving the potato stew to boil, Grandma walked over to the sugar chest and her mind went to Dr. Mayberry. She wondered if he really was a doctor. She wondered if he could have some medicine to relieve her pain and make her feel less tired.

Now why, Grandma thought, should those valley people be so interested in old furniture? This sugar chest wasn't a bit pretty. It was even put together with pegs and plumb worm-eaten and ornery. It could not be materially valuable. Grandma laid her hand on the chest and reflected upon the changes her ninety-odd years had brought and seen. Remembering the story of this sugar chest and the part it had played in her mother's life, brought a smile to her now. She must remember to tell the doctor about that if he came back.

She sat down at her table now and partook of her inadequate meal, a meal that left her unsatisfied in body and rebellious in mind. There seemed something in the atmosphere even bigger than her poverty. Queer, but this thought had not been with her until today. What was it?

Tidying her kitchen, she took her shawl and her pipe and went back to the porch. The sun was slipping over the chimneys now, and shadows lay across her yard. Ezra moved languidly up the steps and, squatting on his haunches, he whined. Grandma pushed at the tobacco in her pipe and regarded the hound, as old and rheumatic for his canine world as she was in hers.

"Ezra," Grandma said, "you've got to stop depending on

me. If it ain't in ye to hunt your own vittles, then you'll have to go somewhere else to live." Ezra answered with his tail and Grandma laughed and went back to the kitchen for the stew leavings. She watched the hound lick the pan clean and then she looked up to see Callie Jenkins turn in at her gate.

"Law, Grandma, that's a hot walk down that road." Callie took off her bonnet and fanned her cheeks.

"What'd ye come fer then, Callie?" Grandma asked, pointing to a chair.

Callie took the chair, then eyed Grandma for several seconds. "I just don't know why I come, Grandma. I been wonderin' about it all the way down the road. I was pickin' turnip greens for dinner tomorrow and somethin' just told me to bring 'em over here to you." Callie dropped the flour sack on the porch.

"I was wishing I had some turnip greens, Callie. I hope ye put in a few turnips, too. They're more tasty that way."

"Ain't ye got a little patch this year?" Callie asked, looking toward the old garden.

"I should a-planted some but just never got around to it," Grandma said. "You heard any kind of news about lately, Callie?"

"Nothin' you don't know already, Grandma. Tom says there's more stew about the land now than common but he don't put no dependence in it much."

"I don't know, Callie. Somehow I don't feel safe up here in the hills no longer. I ain't had a bar on my door ever, for all I been living in this same house for close on to a hundred years."

Callie looked at Grandma and smiled. Folks down her

21

way said Grandma Weller was a little touched in the head, looking off in the distance, chewing on her pipe, and rocking feverishly. Wasn't nothing wrong with Grandma in Callie's mind. No woman ninety years old could midwife better than a real doctor, give out herb medicines to cure man and beast, and still be crazy.

Grandma had a little herb garden she tended herself. Sometimes she went off in the woods, armed with a butcher knife and a basket, and came back with all sorts of roots and barks. After that, you wouldn't see Grandma for days, only the smoke pouring from her chimney. If you were passing, you got a whiff of the orneriest smells. Some of it tasted pretty bad, especially that liver-cleaning tonic, but Grandma had a way of putting in cinnamon and spices so the children would take to the dose a little better. No store-bought medicine in the world could work for coughs and croup better than Grandma's pine tar and honey. There was something else mixed up in it, too, but nobody had ever been able to find out what.

Callie noted now that Grandma looked older and more puny than usual, and it came to her that if Grandma died, it would be the worst thing that could happen in Weller Cove. What would they do without her?

There was Marthy Simmons getting ready to have a baby and Marthy so pindlin' and shaky she didn't have the strength to bring a baby without Grandma's help. Grandma would know what to do when Marthy's time came. Grandma knew everything.

There was old Bud Latham struggling on that hillside farm to pile up enough corn, molasses, and hog meat to last that big family of his through a winter, and Bud having ever' so often the strangest spells that kept him in bed till Grandma went over and gave him a bottle of her tonic. After taking that bottle, Bud would get up, cut himself a hickory limb, and switch every confounded one of his kids till you could hear 'em hollerin' all over the mountain.

Callie went over in her mind the rest of the near invalids within Grandma's range of medical practice, and they were many. They didn't include the well folks, either; folks who got sick when one least expected it. It came to Callie that for all her vibrant health now, she might take to her bed with something most any time.

Grandma sat smoking and regarding Callie with amused eyes. Callie was always worrying about little things and now she was spreading her mind wide open for Grandma to read. That's what came of being old, it gave you a knowledge of things never spoken, knowledge of facts before they even happened. Grandma felt herself able to bring some things about by just thinking them. The proof of that was before her right now. Hadn't she willed Callie to come to her house this very day?

Grandma probed deep into Callie's eyes now and saw her thoughts, which, as in all things human, swung back to Callie herself, demanding from the future what Grandma had given her in the past. She watched Callie stand to her feet now, and begin to tie her bonnet under her chin.

"You ain't going, Callie?" she asked. "Why, I been setting here watching you and it appears to me that yellow look around your eyes might be jaundice, liver or something. Wait here and I'll bring ye a bottle of tonic to clear it up."

Callie reacted just as Grandma knew she would. The

23

hand that reached for the bonnet strings came to suspended movement and in her eyes there was first surprise
and then alarm.

"It's worse than I thought," Grandma said. "You'd better stay all night with me. I'll have you feeling pert in the
morning."

Callie needed no further urging. Tom was away from
home, anyway. He had gone to the valley to check up on
the rumors that the Government really was coming into
the cove and move the folks out. Tom had told her not to
say anything to Grandma to upset her needlessly. There
was time enough when the rumor proved to be a fact.

While Grandma went for the medicine, Callie walked to
the edge of the porch. The sun was behind the ridge now,
and the hollow below the road was dark with shadows. A
squirrel barked from a tree at the edge of the clearing.
Somewhere near, the call of a whippoorwill echoed mourn-
fully in the growing darkness. Callie shivered. She felt a
part, and yet not a part, of the world around her. Once she
talked with Grandma about it and although Grandma's
reasoning sounded simple, it did not fit into Callie's feelings at all.

"Grandma," Callie had said. "I hear everything. I hear
the partridges making nests in the field. I hear music in the
wind. I hear the falls roaring and I even hear the dust
when it rises to a whirlwind in the road. Not an owl at
night but I know when it hoots. It scares me, Grandma."

"It's a good sign when a woman has strong feelings,"
Grandma had told her. "It's the sign of matin' in you. It's
a sort of comfort God sends to make up for other things.
Take hold of it for comfort and don't turn your back,

24

afraid. You'd be surprised the learnin' it brings. There's pockets in women's hearts nothing else can fill; not a husband, not children, and not the work they do. It's a gift. Why, I can even hear corn growin' late in the evening."

"Why, Grandma!" Callie laughed.

"You doubt me?"

"Oh, no. I never doubted you in anything. Just seems sorter funny is all, hearin' corn grow."

Grandma sniffed. "It ain't no funnier than hearin' dust risin' in the road. You start telling that around and folks will think you're crazy. You tell half what you think and know to ordinary folks and, first thing you know, they'll skeeter around you like you was a snake. There ain't a person in a thousand has a mind of his own."

That night Grandma stood in the doorway of her cabin speculating on the weather as was her habit.

"Red glow in the sky, Callie," she said. "Going to be fair and hot tomorrow. Wouldn't be a-tall surprised if a lot of folks don't take sick with this dry spell."

Callie called weakly from the bed. "You reckon so, Granny?"

"Yep," she said, "I do. And after that will come the rains, and then folks'll be gettin' sore throats, the kids the measles and the whooping cough and no telling what else."

Grandma smiled to herself and almost cackled out loud at the way she had willed Callie to visit her on this day, over Callie's falling right into her hands with the jaundice.

"Jaundice!" Grandma sniffed. Callie Jenkins was as healthy and as strong as a cow. Never was sick a day in her life. But Callie was sick now, but only because Grandma had given her something to upset her stomach and make her sick. In the morning she would give Callie a physic and she'd forget all about it.

But in the morning Callie didn't forget all about it. She felt well again, but this transition from illness back to a world of well-being only proved the absolute need of Grandma Weller in her life.

"Grandma," she said, "it's just a sight what you can do with roots and herbs. Makes me plumb uneasy for fear something will happen to you sometime and nobody knowing a thing about your medicines or nothing. It's a gift from God, that's what it is and it ain't Christian for you to keep yourself in!"

Grandma sniffed. "I reckon God didn't lead me to the woods, Callie, and keep me for seventy years speculating with one root and another. It's a wonder I ain't dead, trying out the mixtures on myself."

Callie was horrified. "You mean you even try out the beast medicine, too, like that hog-cholera stuff?"

"Why, shore. A hog is a livin' thing, ain't it? Besides, folks has cholera, too, sometimes. I wouldn't be a bit surprised if a person couldn't take cholera from a hog."

Callie wondered if it was the things Grandma said or the way she looked at her that made her uneasy. In all the time past she had only to come to Grandma to have all her troubles lifted from her. If it was illness, Grandma had the healing ready. If it was worry, Grandma explained it away. Why, thought Callie all at once, Grandma was worried herself, that's where the trouble lay. Maybe she had come to realize her age and frailties and, in her wisdom, she saw death. A feeling of love mixed with pity flooded Callie's heart.

26

"Grandma," she said, "I'm goin' to bring you over some things, we got plenty of everything." Callie's eyes swept the empty shelves, covered the bare floors, looked through the open cracks near the chimney, and came back to rest on Grandma with pity so glaringly evident that Grandma rose to her feet in righteous wrath.

"Don't you get to feelin' sorry for me, Callie Jenkins!"

"Why, Grandma! I just wanted to show ye . . ."

Grandma reached in her apron pocket for her pipe, and her fingers trembled as she poured out the tobacco. She had been a bit hasty in that last remark to Callie. She had meant for Callie to do the things Callie expressed, but in a different way and attitude.

"Callie," she said, "you'll be hearing some things soon that'll surprise you, no doubt. I reckon I might as well come out with it right here and now and get it over with. Nobody's going to give me anything. If they want to pay for what they owe, I ain't against accepting, and this goes for you and Tom as well as all the rest." Grandma lifted a stove lid, took a pine splinter, and lit her pipe, looking at Callie through the smoke she blew out in short, gusty puffs.

Callie smiled, her nervous tension gone with understanding a situation that was no longer a puzzle. Yet she knew Grandma well enough to know that this was something not easily managed. She wouldn't make any more offers until she talked with Tom.

"I reckon I'd better be going, Grandma," she said.

"I can't use my fingers sewing like I once did, Callie," Grandma said. "I hanker for a star quilt like you made last winter, one with three pounds of cotton."

27

Grandma smiled as she noted Callie's reaction. Callie was no doubt thinking of quilt-making in the summer time. Three pounds of cotton made a warm and heavy quilt.

"Don't go to shirking in your mind, Callie," Grandma said now. "When you young folks go to buying cotton off the store counters, already picked and rolled flat in layers, you might as well just tell 'em to roll some goods around it and hand you a made quilt and be done with it."

Callie laughed.

"I'll make you the quilt, Grandma. I ain't never seen a store quilt already pieced and made, but I mind now seeing one in the mail-order catalogue."

Grandma regarded Callie first with surprise, then with humor.

"Is that a fact?"

Callie nodded.

"It beats me," Grandma said, "how I know things without knowing them. You reckon them Government fellers really is coming in and move folks out?"

Callie was remembering her promise to Tom and yet she knew for all Grandma was old enough to die, she was sensible.

"That's what everybody is sayin', Grandma. Tom's gone to the valley to find out if it's so." Callie felt better now for having told. "Don't you worry none, Grandma. Me and Tom is standing by you."

3

THE SUN was just dropping behind the trees when Grandma called from the side yard.

"Chick, chick, chickee-chickee! Better come running, Daisy. One of these days I'll get a hankering for some dumplings and that'll be the end of you."

The wet cornmeal was a surprise to the hungry chickens. They squawked and fought with such clamor around Grandma, she did not hear the wagon on the road.

"Granny!" Jed Simmons threw the line over the gatepost and sped across the yard. Grabbing the feeding pan from Grandma's hands, he dumped the contents into the air and began to push her toward the wagon.

"Wait a minute now, Jed." Grandma disengaged herself and hobbled toward the house.

Jed stared for a second and then rushed over to her. "My Gawd, Grandma! Marthy's time's here and unless ye hurry, no tellin' what'll happen."

Grandma seated herself on the back steps, wearily. "I'm a-feared I ain't able to do no more doctorin', Jed. I'm gettin' old, and bein' out in the night air pains me a lot."

"Good Gawd Almighty, Grandma! Didn't ye hear me tell ye Marthy's time has come? There ain't nobody else can bring her baby but you. You got to go! Hurry up!"

"Ain't ye workin' for them timber folks now?" Grandma asked.

"Of course. But what's that got to do with it?"

"It's got this much to do with it, Jed. I ain't going to make that trip and do that doctorin' for nothing. You can pay me three dollars right here and now if it means that much to ye."

Jed was struck dumb in his tracks. Why, nobody on the mountain ever paid neighbors for helping each other. It wasn't right and he told Grandma so.

"All right! All right!" Grandma cried out. "I've had my say and there it is." Lifting her skirts, she went through the door of the lean-to and began to rattle the stove lids.

Jed followed and stood watching. He just couldn't understand it. Maybe folks were right about Grandma being queer and a little crazy. Suddenly, he thought of Marthy writhing in pain, her cries growing weaker. Reaching into his pocket, he counted out three dollars and laid them on the table.

"You hurry up now, Grandma. This ain't right and I'm going to tell folks about it but I ain't in no place now to argue."

Grandma smiled, slipped the money down the spout of the old teakettle, reached for her wraps and bags, then closed her door behind her.

The ride to the Simmons place was made in silence and like no ride Grandma had ever made. Jed spent his anger on the mules, using his whip the entire three miles, and Grandma wrapped her arms about her body and tried to soften the shock to her throbbing shoulder.

Time and again her glance went to Jed and she found herself comparing him with Aaron Biggers. She didn't know which was worse—Aaron's miserly dealings or Jed's shiftlessness and drunkenness. Aaron worked as hard as any man on the mountain and he, no doubt, had more to show for it in money than any of the neighbors, but what good did it do? His family suffered for lack of clothes to keep them warm in winter; the Biggers family had less to eat than the poorest white trash in the valley.

Jed Simmons worked for only one reason, to get money to buy whiskey. Doubtless he was a part of the crap-shooting crowd that hung out around the falls. Grandma guessed that Marthy had a struggle getting enough to eat for her brood of kids. Homer, the oldest, wasn't but six-teen, and he and Joe, his brother, raised what stuff they did have for the table: a little corn, potatoes, beans, and tomatoes; a few hogs and chickens and maybe a little sorghum.

Grandma's heart softened at the thought of Homer. She hadn't seen him now in nearly a year. He used to come sometimes to bring her gifts; a bushel of meal, a side of bacon, or a couple of squirrels he had killed in the woods. It didn't seem possible for Jed to father a boy like Homer. He was more like Tom Jenkins and Callie.

Here and there along the road, Grandma noticed the approach of winter. Leaves were turning red and yellow, hay was piled high and hanging from the open loft in Aaron's barn. Aaron was feeding his squealing pigs, six of the fattest hogs Grandma ever saw. Her mouth just watered for some spareribs, sausage, and backbone.

"A likely sight," Grandma said.

"Huh!" Jed grunted.

Grandma paid him no mind. Darkness was coming fast now and the night air was sharp like a knife. It crept through her thin clothing like milk through a sieve and she shivered, mumbling to herself.

It came to Grandma that old age with its weakness and frailty had come upon her suddenly. She opposed it, fought against it, and resented it with every ounce of spirit she possessed.

She was disgusted with the young folks, influenced by these summer people from the valley. Nobody was content to work for living comforts any more. They had to have money. And what for? They bought things they did not need and, then, in winter not enough was left to see them through. The old custom of exchanging with neighbors for what each raised was gone and forgotten.

Money was an evil, she thought. Look what it had done to Dave and Jim Pratt. It was bad enough them making liquor for their own use and that of their neighbors. Some of the valley people hit on that liquor, called it mountain dew, and set Dave and Jim up in business. They got them a copper still and paid 'em two dollars a gallon for the stuff. Why, they even built a road back in the hills so they could get the liquor out, hundred gallons at a time. Fine thing that turned out to be, a road. Now these furriners came through in automobiles and even the Government found out they had some more people to boss around, snoop on, and tax for money.

She was jolted out of her reflections when Jed turned the team into the farm lane, the wagon bed rising end up over the wheels, sending Grandma sliding to a quick stop against Jed.

"Here, let me have your hands, Grandma," he said.

"Shut that door, Effie! Ain't you got a bit of sense? Homer! Come get these mules!"

Jed lifted Grandma's ninety pounds to the ground and turned toward the barn.

Stepping into the warm kitchen, Grandma noted with satisfaction the kettles of boiling water. She patted ten-year-old Effie on the head and glanced at the group of smaller children, huddled in the corner. A moan from the next room rose to a thin wail and ended in a piercing scream. Effie put her hands over her ears, her face white and scared.

"She's going to die, Grandma."

"Not yet, honey. Keep plenty of water hot and cook some supper. Folks will be coming in before long."

Clutching her outing bag, heavy with bottles, Grandma opened the bedroom door.

"Stop that carrying on, Marthy!" she roared. "You'd think after seven young'uns, you'd have some sense. Using all your strength to yell, you won't have none left to bring that baby. Here, drink this. In five minutes he'll be tasting it, too, and he'll clamor to get free." Grandma set about making an examination.

"Give me some whiskey, Grandma," Martha begged.

"I'll do nothing of the kind. You take hold of them bedposts and pull, and keep your legs still."

"Oh, Grandma."

"Never mind me, Marthy. You've been through this before and you know how it is. It's different with every woman and your lot is harder than most. You'll have to help me no matter how hard it's goin' to be. Get to work now and keep your mind on your business. You try any faintin' stunts and I'll walk out on ye."

"I can't stand it! I just can't stand it, I tell you."

Grandma seated herself sideways on the bed, propping her shoulders against one of Marthy's knees. "Bear down, Marthy. Bear down hard, honey."

A fit of trembling took hold of Marthy and, growing in intensity, spread to a violent shaking, rocking the bed. Grandma found her own arms tremble, weak with physical effort. She wiped the dripping sweat from her face, mumbling prayers. Time after time she rose, wrung a cloth from a bucket of water, and passed it over Marthy's face, hands, and arms. Grandma tried many remedies but none hastened the birth. As time went on, Marthy grew weaker and no matter how loud Grandma's voice nor how urgent her tone in calling advice, calling for co-operation, the figure on the bed struggled less and less. Marthy was no longer able to bring her baby by herself.

Holding a full glass of gunpowder mixture, Grandma struggled to lift Marthy's head from the pillow. Talking softly, urging and pleading, her voice penetrated the darkness that enveloped Marthy, and though some of the mixture spilled to the pillows, half of it slipped down Marthy's throat. She groaned, and Grandma leaned over the bed

34

more hopefully.

"Can ye sniff a little snuff, ye reckon, Marthy?" Even as she asked it, Grandma stuffed it generously up Marthy's nostrils. From somewhere she found the strength to meet the emergency of birth and delivery. When the baby's cry echoed in the night, Grandma wrapped it in her apron with one hand and reached for the whiskey bottle with the other.

"Here, honey. Drink it all down. If it makes ye drunk, all the better."

Later, Grandma lifted the whiskey bottle again and poured for herself a generous portion. Holding the wailing baby to her breast, she stumbled through the doorway and sought the fireside. She was aware that when she stepped into the kitchen, talk ceased. The small room was full of neighbors and, in the firelight, she saw at least a dozen faces back in the shadows.

"Well," spoke Wade Turner, "supposin' the Government does take over the mountain. They're plannin' to pay us more money than any of us ever seen before. I reckon we can buy us some pretty good farms in the valley."

"I heard some fellers up to the lumber mill say the Government is plannin' to swap us from one farm to another, only it'll be in the valley."

This remark from Jed caught Grandma dangling an outing bellyband before the fire. So, the doctor was right after all. The Government was going to take over the whole mountain and move folks out. And this right when she had all her plans for future comforts clear in her mind. Why, it wasn't just. She had a deed to her land and the

35

Government nor nobody else could take it away from her!

Grandma wrapped the new baby in a cotton blanket, then leaned back and began to rock. This rumor of twenty years, Grandma had never taken seriously. She wondered now at the talk going on around her. There was even an eagerness in the voices of these neighbors of hers, seeing this wholesale selling out as something to look forward to.

She considered for a moment a plan to rise and face them, calling on them for loyalty, a hanging together to maintain their rights, protect the homes of their fathers, preserve the land for their children. But, what arguments could she use? And how could she make them listen to her? These men were two generations removed from her day. If she told them of the hardships of the old days—the long winters of trapping, the isolation, the garnering of food, the weaving of cloth, the spirit that had held the people together by a need of each other—they would only laugh at her.

No, Grandma thought, the Government wasn't taking over now. They had moved in years before, instilling a poison of laziness and greed, so that this final act of buying the land met no opposition. There was nothing she could do about it.

Let them move out if they wanted to. Let them all move out and leave her on the mountain by herself. She wouldn't care. And she wouldn't starve, either. She'd plan now on getting a cow some way, and maybe a litter of pigs. She'd get along.

"I reckon," said Jed, "when us folks gets down to the valley, we'll have a real doctor takin' care of our ailments, not an old woman with a bag of herb bottles and carryin' a gun."

"Yeah," spoke up Aaron, "that's right, Jed. Doctors in the valley have to own a license to go round curin' people. Wonder how some folks'll make a livin' in the valley?"

A general laugh went over the kitchen, following this remark, and rising from her chair, Grandma faced them all.

"So that's how it is, eh? Well, let me tell you something, Aaron Biggers, and all of you. You can just depend on them furrin doctors from now on. I don't work for nothin' any more than you go around givin' away yore meal, Aaron; nor more than you chop down trees for nothin', either, Jed."

Grandma stood for a second but no one answered her. She walked then into Marthy's room and slipped the new baby under the covers.

"You all right now, honey?" Grandma leaned over the bed and patted Marthy's cheek. Marthy nodded and reached out a hand.

"Grandma, I heard what they said. I don't know what's come over Jed. Looks like money is the only thing means anything to him now. He wouldn't take time to plant turnips and expects Homer and Joe to gather all the corn and hay. Homer ain't but sixteen, Grandma, and he's so little and pindlin'. He's tired all the time. Jed's always a-beatin' on Homer."

Martha began to cry weakly.

"Don't fret, honey. It's bad for the baby and you, too. I'll leave a tonic here on the dresser for Homer, and

37

Marthy, if you don't get along all right, send Homer after me some day when Jed's up to the camp. What he don't know won't hurt him. And you'd better stay in bed a week this time, unless you want the next baby to be the end of ye."

Marthy groaned and closed her eyes. Setting herself against Jed was like facing the side of a mountain.

Gathering her possessions, Grandma walked back to the kitchen and once more faced silence following a broken conversation.

"Effie," she called, "fix me a sack of vittles! And Jed, I'm ready to go home."

Nobody said a word. In fact, the only sound to be heard was the scraping of Jed's chair as he tipped back to smile balefully at Grandma.

"All right!" Grandma announced, "I'll fix my own supper and I reckon I ain't forgot how to rope a mule, either. You can come after that mule when ye get good and ready, Jed."

Grandma walked over to the safe and took a couple of soggy corn pones, a baked sweet potato, and a hunk of boiled bacon. Then she reached to the top shelf and helped herself to a half slab of salt pork and a quart jar of blackberry jam.

"Hey!" said Jed, walking over. "What's this?"

Grandma paid him no mind whatever. She lifted her apron and tied the entire lot of food close to her waist. That done, she stepped to the hearth, spat on the fire, then walked through the door, closing it behind her.

If it warn't fer Marthy, she thought, I'd a-slammed that door till it fell off the hinges!

38

The night air settled over her, wet and foggy, and the pain in her shoulder slipped down her arm like a branding iron. She leaned against the house wall, weak and shivering, reaction setting in. Her outstretched hand came back wet and chilled.

"Rain," she mumbled. "Winter jest around the corner."

Holding a hand in front to protect herself, she stumbled through the darkness in search of the barn.

"Grandma," a voice called softly in the night.

Grandma stopped and a small body crept close to her.

"Oh, it's you, Homer. Your pa send ye to take me home?"

"No, Granny," the boy answered. "Aaron said to let you set out in the barn for a spell to cool off. Said he'd take you home when he got good and ready."

Grandma grunted.

"Don't you worry none, Granny. Ma told me to stay with you in the corncrib and to get some gunnysacks for your feet. Ma said tell you onions are drying in the crib along with the taters. I'll ride over with a sack soon's Pa leaves home." Homer shivered in his thin overalls.

"Wish we had a lantern," she said, crawling into the corncrib.

"Best not," Homer suggested. "Be just like Pa to come snooping around, so you couldn't get no taters or onions. Here, Granny, let me help you."

Homer produced a gunnysack and, guided by the smell, Grandma began to pull bunches of onions from the walls.

"Yore mammy tell ye to do this, Homer?" she asked.

"No, but that's what she meant. What's the difference, Grandma? I raised this stuff myself. Pa didn't have nothin'

39

to do with it. He don't work at nothing, lessen it's money he's gettin'. Every week he goes over to Pratt's and comes home so drunk he beats hell outta us kids. The son of a bitch!"

"Homer! That's no way to talk. I'm plumb surprised at ye."

"Maybe not, Grandma, but all the same, if it wasn't for Ma and the young'uns, I'd run off most any day now. Sometimes, Grandma, the feeling in me gets so strong I'm afraid some day I'll just up and run off, anyhow."

"Where would ye go, honey?" Grandma asked. "You likin' this idea of moving to the valley?"

"Hell, no," Homer answered. "Oh, I might like to go down for a spell and see what it's like, Grandma, but I wouldn't stay."

"You'd have to stay if yore pa moved to the valley, Homer."

"Nobody has to do anything they don't want, Granny, not if they got a little gall. I've been hearing things in all this talk. Seems down in the valley the law is pretty strong and makes a feller look after his family. They say liquor is easy to get same as up here but it costs more."

"Then ye think Jed can look after your ma and the kids and leave you free in mind to run off? Is that what ye been thinkin', Homer?"

"What you hintin' at, Granny?"

Grandma was silent for a time. This was a new Homer. Little though he was in size, the work and responsibility placed upon this oldest of Jed's children had given to the boy a maturity. The short sixteen years of his life had been insecure and now in this moving to the valley, he couldn't

40

find the excitement or anticipation expressed by his father and the neighbors.

This thought brought a rise to Grandma's spirit, a quick beat to her heart. In the least expected places and at the most sudden moment and time, there arose from despair and failure, hope that was like an answer to prayer. In this case, to find in this fourth generation removed from her day, a spirit in Homer akin to her own feelings, well, it seemed well-nigh impossible.

"Homer," she answered, "a person has to do what they think is right, always. It'll bring ye up against trouble and you'll have to fight about it, but if ye know you're right, you'd be surprised how much comfort you'll get. Some things in life you can't change, no matter how long nor how much you fight against it."

Homer laughed. "Grandma," he said, "thinkin' don't do no good with Pa. Best let him have his way. Only thing, I'm not sure I'll string along this time. It all depends."

Grandma was thinking up an answer to this when Aaron called out, "Hey, Grandma. How does it feel in the corn-crib? You want to go home with me, better be spry about it."

"You in such a all-fired hurry as that, Aaron Biggers, then go on by yourself. Ye ought to know by this time that hurrying folks don't get ye nowhere," she shouted back.

Aaron lifted the lantern to peer into Grandma's face. The expression he saw there brought over him a sudden suspicion and he began to swell.

"You needn't think I'm goin' to give ye another sack of meal for any herb bottles or salve, Grandma Weller. I reckon we'll be down in the valley by the time Ophie has

41

her baby."

Grandma grunted and, crawling over the doorsill of the corncrib, she slipped through the night toward Aaron's wagon. She felt around in the back and smiled to herself. Homer had placed her sack of onions and sweet potatoes where she could get to them.

When a mile of the way home had been traveled, Grandma turned to Aaron. "How's Ophie's breakin' out?"

"It ain't no good, that's how it's gettin' along. You jest forgot how to mix and brew, Grandma. Too bad you setting yourself up to make folks do things. Leave us be and we'd took care of ye."

Grandma cackled. "If I was dependin' on you for a livin', Aaron, I'd starve plumb to death. If you ever give anybody anything, I never heard tell of it. You young fellers is mighty high and mighty, Aaron, talkin' of what ye'll do in the valley. Why, ever' one of ye is so green and rawboned, them furriners will take everything ye got before a year passes. And as for you, Aaron, you can't outsmart the folks livin' around here. You've got a lot to learn, and when ye get as old as me, you'll know it don't amount to a row of beans. A warm fire, a roof over yore head, and a goodly amount of food, that's all they is in life, anyhow, and I don't care where ye live, in the valley or on a mountain."

"What, ye mean I can't outsmart nobody around these parts?" Aaron asked suspiciously.

"Didn't ye say that salve didn't cure Ophie's breakin' out? Well, I don't reckon it did. In the first place, it wasn't curin' salve. It was axile grease. That's what you get for being in such an all-fired hurry."

42

When Grandma laughed, Aaron drew in the reins and stopped in the middle of the road. He had a good mind to put her out right here and now, old woman or not.

"Don't get het up, Aaron. Won't do ye no good. Ain't but a half mile and it's almost daylight. Drive on."

Stopping in front of Grandma's gate, Aaron waited while she climbed over the wheels. Gathering her bundles from the seat, she walked around the wagon and pulled a sack to the ground.

"What is that?" Aaron roared.

"Nothin' that belongs to you," Grandma snapped.

4

WHEN AARON whipped up his mules and rode off, Grandma tugged at her sacks and bundles. She made three trips to get them into the house and then smiled to herself as she set the bucket of sorghum under her bed. As she went about putting her food supply away, there came over her a new and strange weariness. She wished she had some coffee. That would set her up right smart after her night's labors. Looked like she couldn't stand what she once did.

She put some wood on her fire and sat down to warm herself. She thought of her new pipe and that Virginny tobacco. She hadn't smoked all night. She sat for some time fingering the pipe and her mind again went to the doctor. "Riddin' o' the pain," she mumbled. Perhaps she had better leave the smokin' be and get in bed for a little. Maybe she could sleep and wake up rested again.

Daylight was creeping through the windows and the

chickens were clucking when she slipped 'neath the covers, clothes and all. She was too tired to take them off, damp though they were. Hours passed and no sleep came to her, only that nagging pain in her arm and shoulder and a cold chill she could not rid herself of, no matter how much cover she piled on.

She wondered if she should stay up in the mountains by herself, after all. She might get bedridden and nobody to care for her at all. "Ethan!" she called.

The door opened and a figure came to the bed.

"I heard you call, Grandma. You sick?" Tom Jenkins looked down anxiously.

"No, Tom," she answered, "I ain't sick. I been up all night bringin' Marthy Simmons' baby. Rode home in the mist, and gettin' wet didn't help my shoulder none. Set down."

Tom lifted a basket to the table and began to take out the contents. "Callie sent ye over some things, Granny. Knowed you'd be over to the Simmons, and Jed most likely wouldn't have nothin' to eat in his house. Here's a stewed chicken, a pone of corn lightbread, a cake, and a sack of coffee. I left a poke o' turnips and greens on the porch."

Grandma's eyes lit up with relish at mention of coffee. She hadn't seen coffee in three months.

"Listen, Granny. I'm goin' over to the store this morning. You want I should git ye anything? Sugar, coffee, or maybe a little tea?"

"Well, now, Tom, that's mighty nice of ye. I'm plumb out of sugar and tea." Tom leaned over and took Grandma's hand.

"You remember bringing me, Granny?" he asked.

Grandma nodded, wondering.

"Ye remember the time I had pumony and ye pulled me through?" She nodded again.

"I'm rememberin' a lot of other things, Granny, times you've done things fer me and Callie. It's no use fer ye to try hidin' anything from us, Grandma. I know how things be with you. But they ain't goin' to be that way no longer. I don't want you should be beholdin' to nobody around here nor goin' out nights doctorin' any more."

Grandma lay perfectly still while Tom delivered this unexpected speech, but when he finished, she rose quickly, pushed him away, and touched her feet to the floor.

"Tom Jenkins! When I git to where I have to live off the neighbors, then I'll take Ethan's musket and shoot my brains out," she declared.

"Why, Grandma!" he exclaimed, "I'm downright ashamed of you. Makin' me and Callie beholdin' to you fer all you done fer us over th' years. When we git down in the valley, we'll think of th' debt we owe you and won't be nothin' we can do about it, neither."

"So ye aim to let th' Government walk right over you, too, eh, Tom? Take away the land yore pa and his pa before him slaved on, the house they built and died in. I thought more of ye than that. If I wasn't old and weak, no Government or nothin' else could make me move off my land, lessen I wanted to."

Tom walked over to the hearth and laid a chunk of wood on the fire. That done, he went to the spring for a fresh bucket of water. When he returned, Grandma held the iron kettle while he filled it with water, then she hung it on a crane over the blaze. Coffee was what she wanted most of anything in the world right now. Tom sat before the fire smoking while Grandma fixed her breakfast. When the kettle began to boil, she measured a small amount of coffee, tied it in a bit of cloth, and dropped it in the water.

"Dozen eggs in that basket, Grandma," Tom stated.

"Huh!" she grunted, walking over to the basket to see for herself. She fried a piece of the salt pork she'd got at Jed's, laid it on a plate, dropped the egg in the grease, and then flipped the shells into the boiling coffee. The aroma was so fragrant and tantalizing she could hardly wait. When she sat before the fire nibbling the bacon in her fingers and swallowing the scalding coffee in great gulps, Tom looked on in pity. Why, she was downright starved to death, that's what. He just had to do something about it.

"Listen, Grandma, it ain't a question of the Government takin' a feller's land away from him. It's gettin' more money fer it than it's worth, money that'll buy a farm in th' valley where livin' won't be so hard to make, where ye can sell what ye raise and save for a future. You ought to know what that means, Grandma."

"Yep, I know, Tom. I know how you young fellers feel. Ye can't stand the hardships yore pas had before ye; buying dress goods off a store counter, suits o' clothes already wove and made, soap in a cake that smells like summer flowers. To get down to the bottom of the matter, it's jest money." Granny took another swig of coffee and began to feel strength well up in her, warmth creep through her veins.

"Ye don't think it's th' thing to do then, Granny, movin' to th' valley? Be kinda bad livin' up here just by ourselves with everybody movin' out."

"Why so?" she asked.

47

"Well, in the first place, folks jest can't live to theirselves and get along. There's more in life than just eatin' and sleepin', lovin' and birthin'. Why, that ain't no more than a beast's life, Granny. There's got to be more to work for than jest that."

Tom looked around the cabin. The north foundation had given away some and the cabin had a sort of leaning and out-of-joint look. He could see daylight in chinks through the roof. The one window had two broken panes, and rags were stuffed in the crevices. It had been so as far back as he could remember. Even the big walnut door showed an inch of daylight under the bottom and at the top. Perhaps it was the years of crumbling, but the chimney had lost some of its rocks and dirt-daubed clay and it, too, leaned against the wall, crookedly. Only the floor had improved with age. It was worn smooth and the broad side of the puncheon logs showed clean from Grandma's scrubbing with lye.

His eyes went to the rafters, empty of the customary onion strings, peppers, sage, and bags of herbs. The few clothes hanging on nails near the bed were almost rags. Even the braided rug before the fire had been mended so many times it was a mere scrap, humped and uneven, knotted like a coil of grapevines.

Never until now had her cabin appeared so naked and empty. Grandma had always done for herself, asking help of no one. It would seem that the frailties of old age had come upon her suddenly this past year. The evidence was all around him. She might, as Callie had said, exhibit pride, even in the face of starvation, but to Tom, such a thing now was ridiculous. The time for persuasion was past. No need then to pussyfoot all over the place.

"Look here, Grandma," he said, "it ain't a bit of use to try persuadin' you about goin' to th' valley. You'll have to go whether you want to or not. A lot of folks has already moved out. It's us livin' back in this cove that's slow about it, and that's because them Government fellers hasn't got to us yet. They'll be around most any time now. There's no use settin' yourself agin the Government and lockin' your door against them fellers, Granny." Tom got up and put some wood on the fire, remembering Callie's words: "Better lead up to it real slow and gentlelike."

"Callie and me wants you should go to the valley and live with us, Grandma," he said.

If Tom thought his suggestion had been reached through a tactful and well-laid plan, he was mistaken. Grandma's hand trembled as she filled her pipe. So Tom and Callie really were going to give up and move from the mountain. Only a few minutes before, she had followed Tom's eyes over her empty house, missing none of his thinking. Tom could not know that just the day before, this lack of winter provender had filled her with fear. Grandma's mind went back to the room at Jed's, remembering the talk. If, before, she had reached a sense of security in her plan to charge for her services and so meet her needs, she now knew complete failure. The few weeks left before winter would be hurried, the folks intent on their own affairs, too busy to think of her. The life facing them in the valley was a life that did not include her.

Tom and Callie were the only ones on whom she had set any dependence. Now, they, too, had failed her. The result of Callie's visit had led to this, an offer to pick her up and

49

set her down beside a fire in a strange land, with plenty to eat, warm clothes to wear, and, finally, a coffin and a decent burial. It was as easy as that, like turning an old mare loose in a pasture. A few more months and no one would even remember her. That all her years should lead to this, an acknowledgment of her dependence, taking from her the pride which those years had justly built, she could not accept. Grandma looked at Tom now and suddenly she had a new thought.

"I reckon you'd like me to sell to the Government, git the money, and give it to you, eh, Tom?" She reached for the dishes and started for her kitchen.

Tom leaped to his feet and grabbed her arm. "Now you look a-here, Grandma Weller! Nobody ever accused me of anything dishonest. Callie said you'd take on like that, said you'd make them very words. Well, I done all I can fer ye. I showed ye how to put yore money in th' bank, where ye could get it out when ye wanted anything. I've tried to tell ye that livin' with me and Callie, so we could do fer ye when ye get sick and ailin', is a thing we want to do because we're rememberin' the years you done for us." Tom reached for his hat and, walking to the door, he turned and spoke in hurt tones. "Grandma, I reckon you're the only person on the whole mountain who thinks me a thief."

Tom picked up the reins and called to his mules, looking back toward Grandma's house. It was the only cabin on the whole mountain that remained as built, over a hundred years ago. Other homes had undergone changes—a tin roof to replace old handmade shingles, here and there a new rock chimney held together with cement instead of clay, plank floors instead of the old puncheon logs, an extra window here and there for light. That cabin of Grandma's couldn't be more than sixteen by twelve. That lean-to at the back had practically separated itself from the house, leaning off like a privy. At the thought of a privy, Tom looked toward the stretch of woods a hundred yards from the cabin and thought of Grandma stumbling through snow and ice in winter.

The stubborn old heifer! Made him so consarned mad he didn't know what to do. He was a good mind to lay the matter before them Government fellers and get them to make Grandma move out. She wouldn't last out another stretch of winter. If he couldn't do it no other way, he'd slip up some day when she was off doctorin', and burn the gol-derned place to the ground. He'd have to burn that rickety barn, too, and fill the cellar with dirt. Give her a hole big enough to crawl in and she'd hold on to that cussed pride to the last. Like as not, she'd take that old rusty musket and shoot somebody sure as Gawd.

Tom drew the team to the side of the road as a car approached. These mules of hissen were as stubborn as old Grandma Weller, rising up on their hindlegs, a-kickin' and a-fumin' at the least strange noise or disorder.

"Whoa!" he shouted, as a car stopped and Dr. Mayberry motioned to him with a hand.

"Hello, Tom," the doctor called out. "You know if Grandma Weller is at home?"

Tom sat on the wagon seat, fingering the reins, wondering if he should tell Dr. Mayberry about this bothersome situation. Perhaps as a valley man, the doctor might have a suggestion.

"Grandma's home, Doc, but she's in a awful temper.

Kinder sick, too. She's been up all night bringing Marthy Simmons' baby. Look, Doc, what can a feller do with an old woman like Grandma?"

"What do you mean, Tom? Is the old lady appealing for help?"

"Good Gawd, no! Grandma Weller would starve plumb to death before she'd let ye know she was in need. That pride of hers is a hide of chestnut burrs."

Dr. Mayberry smiled, remembering his last visit with Grandma. "Tell me about it, Tom."

"Doc, it would take all day to tell ye about Grandma Weller. She's th' only old settler left up here now. We ain't never had a doctor come in this cove for anything. It goes way back before my time. Ma used to tell me a lot. There ain't a family in miles of here that don't owe a life to old Grandma. Some of her medicines and tonics travels over fifty miles from here and to folks she never saw. She never set her foot inside a church up here and yet, in times past, I reckon her word had more to do with our livin' than the preacher's that came and went."

"A sort of ruler of the mountain, in ways?" the doctor asked, smiling.

"Yep, that's it. And th' folks couldn't a-got by without her, neither."

"And now they are all moving to the valley and Grandma has found she isn't needed any more. That it?"

"Yep, I guess that's it. Callie and me talked it out last night. Our folks owe more to Grandma than we could ever pay back. What I can't make her understand is that doing for her now that she's old and useless is something we want to do. Why, Doc, she ain't got enough grub in her house to last a week, and winter just a few weeks off. She's scared to death and thinks I don't know it."

"Can't the folks get together and provide food for her winter?" Dr. Mayberry suggested.

"Grandma set out to charge for her services of late and now some of the folks are rising up against her. You see, she never charged nothin' before. Mountain folks is strong for habit, Doc."

Dr. Mayberry stepped out of his car and stood by the wagon. "You said something then, Tom. Mountain folks are strong for habit. It is the real old ones that can't change. Grandma's years are a pattern that she has found suddenly to be completed."

Tom was silent for a minute, considering the doctor's words. "I hadn't thought like that, Doc. All the same, when everybody moves off the mountain, Grandma can't stay up here by herself. I don't know what I'm goin' to do 'cause I can't go off and leave her and she won't go with me and Callie. I'm worried, Doc, I sure am. Whoa, ye confounded ignoramus!" The offside mule was sidling toward the woods, kicking and biting.

"Doc, I'll have a hell of a time gettin' that mule down th' mountain. The son-of-a-gun's so all-fired green he rises up like Grandma Weller agin anything that ain't natural to him."

The doctor threw back his head and laughed. "I've been thinking about you, Tom. I was on my way today to your place. How would you and Callie like to run a farm of mine in the valley?"

"I don't get you, Doc," Tom said.

"I have a good farm lying alongside the river. I'd like to

take you down to see it. If the place appeals to you, then we'll talk terms. I don't believe you could find land that would suit you better."

"Well. . . ." Tom hesitated.

"No decision now, Tom. I'll be by tomorrow at nine o'clock. You and Callie be ready. By the way, I've been wondering how Grandma kept up the taxes on her place, Tom."

"Nobody knows, Dr. Mayberry, and I don't want 'em to know, especially Grandma. But my pa before me paid the taxes on her place and af'er he died, I paid 'em."

"Must have been hard at times to pay taxes on two places."

"You're right, it was. Money is hard to come by up here. I've had to plant more corn and sell it to Dave Pratt for making whiskey. I've sold vegetables to the folks over at the settlement and Callie has sold a number of quilts. Me and Callie didn't mind."

The doctor drove off, and Tom turned the team in the middle of the road and headed back home.

5

WHEN DR. MAYBERRY stopped his car in front of Grandma's cabin, he lifted out a basket and a leather case. These in his arms, he walked up the path and knocked on the door. Ezra ran out, sniffing at his legs.

"Well! Come on in! You want I should lift the latch?"

The doctor smiled, full of humor, and walked into the cabin.

"Howdy, Doc. Didn't know it was you. Wouldn't have been so quick. Pull up a chair and set. Fire feels sorter good this morning." Grandma shifted in her rocker, holding to her shoulder. "Seems I took cold in my shoulder, Doc. Got a onion poultice on it to draw off th' pain."

Dr. Mayberry slipped the basket and leather case to the floor and sat there, studying Grandma. He sat so long, so quiet, and so contemplative, Grandma grew restless under his gaze and shifted nervously in her chair.

"Well, go on and say!" she spat out. "I can cure everybody on the mountain, exceptin' myself. It's th' Gawd's truth. I swallered a little of every tonic I make. I even took sulphur and molasses, coal oil and turpentine, mustard and sheep droppings. Then I made poultices o' oak leaves, mustard, bran mixture, and cow manure. Nothin' does any good. Was outta onions till today."

Dr. Mayberry leaned over and opened his case. Taking out a stethoscope, he drew up close to Grandma.

"What is that?" she asked, pushing back.

"Now, now," the doctor placated. "Don't tell me you've been doctoring people for sixty years and never used a stethoscope, Grandma. I have an old one here I brought you."

Grandma leaned over to examine the instrument. "What's it for?"

"Suppose you put these little ends in your ears and listen to my heart and chest, Grandma, then maybe you can tell me what it's for."

The doctor bared his chest, guided her hand, slipping the instrument over his chest, breathing deeply and long. He watched the interest creeping into her eyes. Suddenly, Grandma grasped at the stethoscope, holding it close.

"Why, Doc, that's just wonderful! Where in the world did ye get it?"

"Oh, that's just one of a lot of inventions the valley folks have, Grandma. I'd like mighty well for you to see my hospital."

"What for?"

Dr. Mayberry spent a half hour explaining hospitals, routine, and physical examination to Grandma. There were times when she seemed suspicious and doubtful but she did not fuss or oppose when the doctor offered to give her an examination. Some parts of the examination she felt to be indecent and downright unnecessary but seeing the look on the doctor's face, she made no objections.

Finally, Dr. Mayberry leaned back in his chair, looking into the fire while Grandma buttoned her dress over her bosom and drew her shawl around her shoulders. She eyed him fearfully, afraid of what he might say. Then, as minutes went by and he did not speak, it came to her that he had no curing medicine for what ailed her after all, possibly did not even know what was wrong with her. She could well understand the latter and not blame the doctor one bit. She had seen people die. She had treated them for one thing and another and they still died.

"I guess it's just old age a-creepin' up, Doc," she suggested. "I reckon it's about time fer me to be ailin', full of stiffness and pain."

"How old are you, Grandma?" he asked.

"I don't just exactly know, Doc. I remember the big trees here in the yard, the animals Pa killed and skinned fer fur. I remember how hard it was to raise chickens on account of the foxes. Why, it was so bad in th' woods then, it warn't safe to get out after dark. Ma was from a town in No'th Ca'lina and she couldn't get used to th' woods. I remember how lonesome she got and how she cried when the hoot owls roosted near the house. But Ma learned a lot before she died. If hoot owls ever bother you, Doc, jest git up and turn yore shoes upside down under th' bed and they'll stop right away."

Dr. Mayberry laughed.

"It's th' Gawd's truth, Doc. I guess I could tell ye a lot o' things ye don't know, things ye wouldn't believe no doubt, fer all they're so."

"I'm sure you could, Grandma. I'd like to know about the old days. Other people would, too. Wish you could write it all down in a book."

Grandma laughed. "Shucks! Nobody around here'll even listen to what folks once did, the way they lived. Why, they even laugh. Makes me feel bad, too. Why, there ain't a half-dozen folks on this mountain now with a tenth th' gall it took to live in th' old days." Grandma sat back in her rocker and looked into the fire. "They were good days. I wouldn't trade 'em for now."

"What to you is the biggest change, Grandma?"

"Well, I reckon it's th' lack of neighbors and th' need of each other. I think a lot about you valley folks, how you git along by yourselves, don't need no help from each other. Wouldn't be a-tall surprised if a time don't come when all that's changed. Folks can't go on livin' to theirselves and prosper. Makes me think of my own ma. Got time to listen?" she asked.

"Sure thing," he answered.

"I never told this story to nobody before. Folks who know it are long since gone. I reckon I'll sort of mix it up in the telling but it's my ma comin' from outland places, like you valley folks live in, that makes me wonder about your ways. Wagon trains used to go across the mountains, taking stuff to the folks over in Kentucky. Pa jined this wagon train to be safe. A wagon like that don't hold much, but seems Ma just would hold on to her sugar chest and all th' time it was full of sugar. Pa fussed and said there warn't

58

no room fer such foolishness in the wilderness, but Ma cried and wouldn't go without the chest. She said so long as it stood full of sugar, then she wouldn't fear starvation and her house would be looked up to among the settlers.

"First off, the neighbors fer miles around come in and helped Pa to raise this house, log by log. Ma just set off to th' side, her hand on that sugar chest, crying. Some women folks brought baskets of grub and laid out dinner on th' ground. They tried to make friends with Ma and all she'd do was open that chest and show 'em her sugar. Some of them women never saw white sugar before. Once one of 'em reached out a hand to taste and Ma pushed her hand back.

"After that, the women left Ma alone with her sugar chest. They said she could be high and mighty all by herself. Sometimes Pa would be away for days at a time and just Ma and me at the cabin. Before it was good and dark, she'd bar the door and th' winder and then huddle with me by the fire. And outside in the night the animals would prowl close, th' wolves and painters and even bears coming in. We could hear 'em scratching around the door. Next morning, no matter how much care, some of th' chickens would be gone. One morning we saw a bear come out of the pigpen carrying a half-grown pig. Ma grabbed Pa's old musket, opened the back door, and shot that gun in the direction of that bear. I remember Ma shut her eyes when she pulled th' trigger and the blast knocked her flat on her back on the floor."

Dr. Mayberry laughed. "She killed the bear, I suppose?" he asked.

"Gawd Almighty, no! She killed th' pig."

"And that scared the bear off?" The doctor was helping Grandma along with her rambling story, wondering how the sugar chest figured in it. "Don't rush me, Doc. I'm tryin' to show ye how hard it was to live in them days. As to th' bears, it took more than a gun shot to scare 'em off. That blast from Ma's gun knocked th' pig to th' ground and that bear jest looked over to th' house and thanked Ma for helpin' him out. Then he picked up that dead pig and walked off in th' woods."

Dr. Mayberry rocked with laughter.

"Now, about that sugar chest," Grandma went on. "It was on that very day that Ma had a baby and nobody there but just us. Pa was due back in time for that baby, but I reckon that bear scare brought it early."

"How old were you then, Granny?"

"About nine, I reckon. That was th' start of my doctorin'. Th' way Ma depended on me was a sight. I had to make out like nothin' scared me on account of Ma."

"And you delivered your mother's baby at such an age?"

"I just watched it come and done what Ma told me to do, Doc. Trouble was, Ma fainted and there I was by myself with that baby in all that mess, not knowin' what to do with it."

"What did you do, Granny?"

"Well, I stood there by th' bed for a while, watchin' it turn blue, then, when the afterbirth come, I got some shears."

Dr. Mayberry shuddered. "My God," he muttered.

"Then, when Ma come to herself and cried out, I held th' baby up fer her to see and she yelled and laid back again all quiet. I wrapped th' baby in a quilt then, and laid it on a chair and then I burned some of the covers in the fire like Ma told me to do. When Pa came home that night, he said th' baby was dead. Looked like Ma would never get her strength back after that. She told Pa to bury th' baby under the hollyhock roots in the yard, but it come such a freeze and th' ground was so hard, Pa couldn't dig a hole. So he hid th' baby under the hay in the barnloft and didn't tell Ma."

"I suppose he buried it later on when a thaw came," Dr. Mayberry prompted.

"Wasn't nothin' to bury by that time. The rats had et the baby right down to the rags it was wrapped in, so Pa buried the rags." Grandma looked over at Dr. Mayberry, smiling at his expression.

"Why, that ain't nothin' a-tall, Doc. There's much worse things come about on this mountain, back in them years."

"And the sugar chest?" he reminded her gently.

"Oh, yes. Well, it took years of lonesome living for Ma to see it was the sugar chest that kept folks away. She learned that a woman couldn't live in a wilderness all by herself with nobody to help in time of need. There come a winter when all the salt give out and folks watched and watched the trail for a wagon train. You see, them trains brought salt to th' folks in the mountains and traded it for other things. Now, on this particular winter, salt got so scarce that you couldn't even borrow a pinch to make hoe-cake. Folks couldn't kill their hawgs for winter meat and it was even risky to kill wild game.

"It got mighty bad around a Christmas. I remember going with Ma, once, to a neighbor-woman's house when Ma tried to trade a cupful of sugar for just a pinch of salt

61

fer bread. That woman laughed in Ma's face. Pa dug up the dirt under the smokehouse and Ma boiled it down to about a quart of brown salt. We et that salt from our hands just like it was sugar, only it tasted a lot better than sugar."

"What happened to the wagon trains?" Dr. Mayberry asked.

"Why, it was the war going on, Doc, the Civil War. When a time come, finally, and not even a spriggin of brown salt was left, it got so Ma couldn't swallow a bite of food. You have to go a long time eatin' fresh meat without salt to understand it, Doc. Pa got on his horse one day, saying he wouldn't be back till he brought some salt. A week later he rode in with a whole sack, and he had killed a man to get it, a man who had stole that salt himself and from th' Army somewhere in the valley."

"I guess your mother was happy, then, and you killed your hogs."

Grandma laughed. "Nope. Ma sent words fer miles around and the folks rode in to our house. Ma divided that salt, cup by cup. She called the womenfolks in and they started in to makin' pies with the sugar. They used every grain and they danced and partied all night long in this house. Ma never lacked fer neighbors then. She opened that sugar chest and poured in her portion of salt. Never did she use the chest for any other purpose."

"That's a good story, Grandma."

"Yep, I reckon so. Main thing to me, is bein' neighbors. Folks can't get along without each other. Another thing is that sugar ain't very valuable, and salt is. Why, I've went as many as two years without seeing a spriggin o' sugar."

"Molasses?" he asked.

"Sorghum molasses. It grows good in these coves. In the old days, sorghum-makin' time was a treat. People would gather for miles around and sometimes they'd stay all night, beddin' out in the barn and in the woods; the womenfolks and children in the house and on the floors."

"Tell me about it, Grandma," Dr. Mayberry asked.

Grandma laughed. "Doc, I've seen too many such years to garner one right off as bein' the most interesting. You know old Bud Latham's place up the road?"

The doctor nodded. "That's the big log house with the runway through the middle, a tin roof?"

"Yep, that's th' one. Back in his pa's day, the Latham house was a house of plenty and somethin' was allus a-goin' on up there. Lance Latham had fourteen children and they was the workingest kids you ever seen. I guess it was because old Lance used a hickory limb on 'em."

"I guess a family that big had to work hard to get enough to eat, Grandma."

"Well, Doc, back in them days a feller had to work hard, of course; but game in the woods was so plentiful he never lacked for meat. The Latham land was fine plantin' fer sorghum cane, so they raised most that was used in this cove. They traded the sorghum to the neighbors for other things. It was tradin' back and forth in them days. There's a settlement of folks living back of us here, up on Knob Ridge, fine folks, too. Used to be an old man by the name of Lief Tatum. He was th' first white man to settle in these here mountains. Some awful things happened up on Knob Ridge back in the old days. Sometime I'll tell you some of them tales, Doc, and I reckon you won't believe it."

63

"Dr. Mayberry reached over for his case and stood to his feet.

"Oh, no, don't go now, Doc," Grandma said. "You got me talkin' of things that don't matter any more. Set down!"

The doctor laughed, opening his medical kit.

"You got some curin' medicine fer what ails me?" she asked cunningly.

"I've got some tablets here to make you sleep better. A little rest and food for a week and then we'll take out your teeth. That's your trouble, Grandma, poison in your blood."

When Grandma sat back in her chair, saying nothing, holding her shawl with clutched and nervous fingers, the doctor said, "You wouldn't feel it at all, Grandma. Doctors in the valley have some tonic to put in the gums to make the nerves dead for a time."

"I wasn't thinkin' o' that, Doc. I ain't afraid of pain. I'd a-pulled them teeth out myself long ago if I'd had money for some store-bought ones. Sary Greenlaw got her some store teeth. Shore is purty and she can eat better than with her real ones. I been wantin' some of them teeth fer I don't know how long."

Dr. Mayberry was counting out pills in his hand, conscious of Grandma's silence. "As to the expense of the teeth and the doctoring, I'll have to charge you fifty cents for the examination and a dollar for the teeth," he said.

"Oh, no you don't, Doc. Sary's teeth cost twenty-five dollars. She ordered 'em out of a paper. Good Gawd, I ain't seen that much money since Ethan died! I'll have to do without the teeth but, if you want to pull my old ones out,

64

I'll give ye a dollar fer yore trouble."

"How many babies you suppose you've delivered in your time, Granny?" the doctor asked.

"Gawd Amighty, no tellin'! I gave up countin' long ago. Wouldn't be surprised if it ain't five hundred or more."

Grandma rocked quietly in her chair, watching the doctor. She liked him. He was the only person from the valley she had ever liked. He had a kind heart. But why should he go out of his way to help her? What could she have that he would want? Oh, yes, the sugar chest.

"Listen, Doc. About that little old sugar chest. What makes folks interested in old furniture, anyhow?"

"Well, Grandma, there's a craze going around for hand-made furniture like yours. Not much of it is left any more. Most of it is pretty rickety and it takes money to have it done over and polished for use in the valley. It is valuable because it is rare. If I were you, I wouldn't let anybody beat me on the price, that is, if you want to sell yours."

Grandma turned her head, looking over her house. He wanted to make it easy for her and yet, it might be these old pieces of furniture were so much a part of her life, to take them away would be a heartbreak. Still, sooner or later somebody would get them and perhaps cheat the old woman. She was not going to allow anyone to do anything for her free and unhampered. The doctor eyed the cherry spool bed. It was a beauty but must be very uncomfortable for sleeping. Very likely it was rope-slatted and had no springs; just a thick featherbed on top of a shuck mattress. He considered an innerspring mattress, warm woolen comforters, and soft blankets.

"Did your father make this furniture, Grandma?" he

asked gently.

"No, he didn't. Back in the old days there was a feller named Christman goin' around makin' furniture for them that could afford it. He took furs in trade. Christman didn't stay around here but a few years. Most of the folks made their own stuff. It was to make Ma more contented that Pa had things as nice fer her as he could. There's a loft room above. Some stuff is up there now. A piece or two is out in the barn crib. I ain't got no need for it now. That bed, the chest, table, and these two rockers, is all I need any more."

"Then you'd like to trade with me, Grandma?" he asked.

"You don't even know what's up in the loft, Doc. I think you got ideas in your head for some reason." That the doctor was setting out to help her, Grandma was now certain.

"Suppose you tell me what's in the loft, then."

"Oh, stuff that ain't no 'count to nobody, a broken-down table, a chest with one leg off, a cupboard that fits in a corner, some worn-out chairs, a spinning wheel and a loom, and a few old wooden picture frames. Out in the barn is a trundle bed and a cradle."

Dr. Mayberry made a list of the articles as Grandma called them off. He figured for a few minutes, then looked over at Granny who was eyeing him closely. If he offered a just price in money, she might refuse to deal with him. He couldn't allow that, for the old lady was in need, hungry. The doctor preferred to fill her kitchen with food and leave her with her furniture, but someone else would get it from her and cheat her out of its value. He might as well collect it for his wife.

66

"Grandma," he said, "this furniture of yours is worth a truckload of food, from flour and sugar to meat, and your winter's supply of tobacco."

Grandma laughed. "You're a good man, Doc. I know one when I see him. But, I ain't askin' for help from nobody. Anyhow, how you expect me to live without a bed and a chair? I don't know as I could get used to a strange bed and a different sort of chair. This one here just seems to fit for me."

"You keep the chair, Grandma, but I've got a bed to swap you that'll be like sleeping on a cloud. In selling my summer place over at the settlement, I have to move our stuff down to the valley. I'll bring over any pieces you want or need, be glad to."

"But why you doin' all this fer me, Doc? I ain't never done nothin' fer you."

Dr. Mayberry reached for Granny's hand. "Look, Grandma, we have both spent years doctoring folks; me in the valley, and you on the mountain. We understand each other. We understand people and how ungrateful some of them are. Down in the valley, the doctor charges for his services but that does not mean that all the folks pay. But, enough of them pay to support the doctor. You should have charged a long time ago, then folks would have appreciated you more."

"Yep, I reckon you're right, Doc. But if I had the strength I used to have, I wouldn't be thinkin' of all that. I'd rather do for myself. I guess I could a-got by if the Government hadn't come in like this. Seems like I can't understand nor get used to the idee a-tall."

"You plan to stay on? You think that's best?"

"Doc, I'll never leave the mountain. Even if I'm up here by myself, I'll stay. I aim to die in my own house and on my own land."

"Don't blame you a bit, Grandma." Dr. Mayberry reached for his hat, picked up his case, and started for the door. "I'll be back in a week and we'll get those teeth out. Take one of those white tablets at bedtime and get plenty of rest."

Grandma glanced at the floor and saw the basket. She hobbled to the door and called out, "Hey, Doc, you left something."

"It's for you, Grandma, present from me."

The car rolled down the road and Grandma stood in the doorway, thinking. This sympathy and understanding came from an outlander, a man from the valley. She would have to think about all this. She was sure her old furniture was not worth a truckload of food, so she couldn't allow him to give her anything. To get her teeth out was needed and she'd pay him a fee for it.

Grandma walked over to the big basket, full of curiosity. She sat in her rocker eyeing it for a long time. Then she lowered herself to the floor, lifted back the top. It was the prettiest basket Grandma had ever seen, a luncheon hamper and full of strange and wonderful things—knives, forks, spoons, plates, cups, and glasses all red in color and light to the touch. She fingered them reverently. This was a mistake. He didn't mean for her to keep the basket. There was cheese in boxes, a loaf of bread, a sack of coffee, cans of milk, jars of peaches, a box of candy. Grandma sat there fingering the contents until night came on and the chill of the cabin crept into her awareness. She went out to

68

feed the chickens, and to gather bits of wood from the barn lot. Tomorrow she would wake up rested with a new hope in her heart. She would start right away to get ready for winter. There were many things she could do.

6

GRANDMA STOOD by the rail fence, looking over into her old garden patch, wishing now she had made some effort at planting back in early summer. She might have pulled up the old cornstalks, dropped in a seed, and then tramped the ground with her foot. But she kept putting it off, thinking she would feel stronger another day. Somehow, the summer had flown so fast.

What had she been thinking of, anyway, letting these weeks run by and no grub garnered for winter! She had depended on the neighbors to bring things to her when they saw her empty field. Queer, they wouldn't notice these things in passing, and there had been more passing of late then ever before. Everybody seemed in a hurry, too. They used to stop by her gate and talk for a bit, pass on news if nothing else.

This bustle and hurry along the cove road added nervousness to Grandma's fears. Funny, after planning to charge the folks for her doctoring to fill her shelves, there wouldn't be any folks left to be doctored. They would just ride down to the valley, taking their harvest yield with them and without a backward thought of her.

She looked out over the fields, grown dense with samplings and sassafras. When Ethan was here, those fields at this time of year stood full of corn shocks, yellow pumpkins showing bright bellies to the sun. In the barn loft, hay was piled to the rafters, the crib full of the corn. Two fat mules fed noisily in the stalls.

Grandma closed her eyes, holding this vision close to her. She could hear the tinkle of the cowbell in the creek pasture. Far away there came over the air the crack of a rifle, Ethan hunting the hogs in the woods, hogs grown fat on acorns and beech mast.

There was a big iron kettle full of boiling water, the steam rising, a fire crackling underneath. Everything was ready for the butchering, lard making. Piles of hickory wood stood near the smokehouse, ready to smoke the hams and the bacon. The hives had been robbed of the honey, and buckets of sorghum were in the cellar. Cords of wood rose near the chimney. Everything was ready for winter. Winter! Something had to be done about winter.

Grandma walked down to the gate when she heard a wagon on the road. She would try to stop this person, whoever it was. Perhaps they would tell her something with a mite of comfort in it.

It was more than one team on the road. First came Jed Simmons on his mule. He passed Grandma with a half-hearted lift of the hand. Then came Bud Latham on his

71

gray mare.

"Be by in a day or so, Grandma," he called out hoarsely.

Next came a wagon and team with Sam Acree and his wife, Josie. Why, Tom and Callie, too! Grandma stepped out in the road, held up a hand, and Sam pulled the team to a stop.

"Now what's goin' on around here?" Grandma demanded. "Everybody passin' me as if I was a tree. Get out and come in!"

Sam laughed. "We was aimin' to, Grandma."

Grandma led the way to the porch, eagerly. Here was a chance to find out for certain now, just how the land laid with these two families. Sam Acree and Josie came next to the Jenkins in Grandma's affections. She had brought into the world all six of Josie's children.

"Go in the house and get some chairs, Tom," she said, seating herself in her hickory rocker.

"No, we'll just sit on the steps here, Granny. Me and Sam's movin' on in a minute or so. Callie and Josie aims to spend the day, if you want 'em."

"Course I want 'em, but what in tarnation does all this trekin' up and down the road mean? Nobody stops, everybody's in a hurry. I never saw such carryin' on before. They ain't a-movin' off the mountain now, are they?"

"Folks is gatherin' at Aaron Biggers to meet a feller from back on Pine Ridge. This Lige Holder is gettin' the mountain folks to join together and fight th' government in court about th' land."

Grandma stared at Tom. She did not know a person could fight in court over the land. For that matter, she didn't credit the cove folks with the spirit needed to stand together. She was delighted. Perhaps they didn't intend to move off after all, at least not this winter. They would need her after all. They might have the nerve to stand together at the start but when it came to carryin' on, they must have a leader. She got to her feet. These neighbors had come to her now for help and advice just as in the past.

"Well, don't sit around here! Go get my bonnet, Callie, and my shawl. I guess I'll have somethin' to say about sellin' out, too. Nobody around here has got as much land as me."

"Nothin' to it, Granny, and no hurry needed," Tom said gently.

"What's that?" Grandma stood in front of Tom, her hand shaking on her cane. "You mean you're goin' to fall down on the mountain folks, sell out?" she yelled.

Nobody said anything. They just sat there on the porch nervously eyeing Grandma, each afraid to express an opinion.

"Who is Lige Holder, anyhow? Never heard of him. What is he doing around this cove and how come some of you fellers can't stand up to your rights in your own neighborhood?"

Tom and Sam rose, a look passing between them. Tom spoke.

"Lige Holder wants more money for his place than the Government offers. He's mad and says he won't sell for the price. All he's doing is rousing the mountain folks here and there to hold out and fuss, causing them Government fellers trouble. Damn foolishness is all, Grandma."

"I see," Grandma said. "I reckon it's damn foolishness

fer a man to fight fer what belongs to him and what belonged to his folks for over a hundred years and more. Any man in this cove who gives up without a fight, takes up his stuff and walks off, and not a word or a look back toward the home his pa built and died in, then it's a good riddance to th' mountain and I'll be glad to see him leave. That means you, too, Tom Jenkins."

Tom walked down the steps and around the house without a word and Grandma looked at Sam Acree. Sam tried to laugh it off.

"Listen, Grandma, me and Tom was going over to Aaron's just for fun. They say that old Lige is better'n a tent show. He's been travelin' around th' mountain for weeks and seems he gets madder and madder all th' time. Said if nobody jined up with him to fight in court, then he was goin' to load his gun and kill the first Government feller that set foot on his land. Don't you know that ain't no way to do, Grandma? Why, some fellers won't have no more sense than to believe all that talk Lige spits out, and they'll land in jail. I ain't havin' a thing to do with it, and I'm plumb surprised at you. In the first place, who is Lige Holder to come around this cove tellin' us what to do?"

Grandma sat back in her rocker. If only she had called all the cove folks to her house before this Lige Holder happened along. She wondered just what he had to say, how he went about getting people together and organized. She looked over at Callie and Josie and from them to Sam. She was so disappointed in them she could have cried.

"Listen, Grandma," Sam said, "I couldn't do nothin' else with that family of mine. I don't want to move. I lay awake at night thinkin' about it. I've been in the valley before and I know how it is down there, everybody pushing and fightin' each other, beatin' a man out of his teeth if he ain't careful. It's every man fer himself, and work is never done. It's my kids I have to think about, not myself."

"What about yore kids, Sam? Ain't the mountain good enough fer 'em? It was good enough fer yore folks before you and you, too," Grandma chided.

"No school fer th' kids if we stay up here, Grandma, I can't think of just myself, now. Things change so fast it keeps me worried. Only thing a feller can do fer his young'uns is to give 'em a little schoolin' so's they can look after themselves. Me and Josie has talked it out, Grandma. We ain't goin' to fight the move and we ain't fightin' the price offered. It's fair enough."

"Grandma," Josie said timidly. "Come with me and Sam and live with us. We can't get along without your doctorin', all them kids of ours."

Grandma laughed, harshly. So it really was a fact. They were all going to move off and the only thing they could offer her was a home with them. They had talked it over and arranged for her just as if she was a chair or a bed. They knew her kitchen was empty, for Callie had told. Well, it was a joke on them.

Grandma's mind went to Dr. Mayberry's offer to buy her furniture. It was like a prayer answered. Now that she no longer need be afraid for winter provender, there was no reason to seek help from anybody around her. Grandma cast a pitying eye at these weak children before her, spineless remnants of the old days, thin-blooded, not a fighter among them. She looked up to see Tom carrying two pails of water up the hill from the creek hollow.

"What are you up to, anyhow?" she asked, suspiciously.

Callie spoke up. "Me and Josie thought we'd wash your quilts and clothes today, Grandma, and clean your house good fer winter. It's a good day, sun warm and ground dry."

Grandma wanted to rise up and ask them to leave her house and herself, leave her to her own plans and doings. But that was not neighborly in spirit nor was such a thing ever done on the mountain. Besides, they owed her plenty, so why not let them do her chores for her? Best she be thinking of something for dinner, too. What sort of meal she could scare up off those empty shelves she didn't know, but whatever it was, she'd set it out with pride; she would have nobody displaying pity for her.

"Washing the quilts would be a help, Josie. I was aimin' to get to it tomorrow. Guess I'll go back and hatch up a snack."

Callie pushed Grandma back in her chair. "We brought dinner with us, Grandma. When Sam and Josie passed and called out, I jest lifted th' pot of beans off the stove and brought it along, with a tomato pie I made yesterday. You just set here on the porch and we'll get the kettle to boiling."

Time passed and Grandma sat there in her rocker, smoking, hearing the talk and clatter in the side yard. There was the sound of an axe in the hollow below the house and, presently, Sam led a mule down the hill to reappear soon, after dragging a good-sized tree to the yard. There were several of these trips, and then came the sounds of a crosscut saw. They were going to cut stove wood for her. Perhaps if she just sat there and didn't seem

76

to notice, they'd stack a sizable pile for her.

Grandma looked over and saw Ezra sleeping in the sun at the end of the porch, unmindful of the activity going on around him. Poor old Ezra! He wouldn't live through the winter, likely. Maybe Sam would take him to the valley; there would be more to eat down there. Be lonesome without the dog. Seemed like just an animal was comfort in the long days when one must stay in and sit by a fire. Grandma followed Ezra's example and nodded in her chair. She awakened with a start. Hobbling down the steps and around the house, she saw the rail fence hanging full with the washed quilts, clothes, and rags. The kettle was turned on its side, the fire a pile of smoldering ashes. Josie's laugh rang out in the lean-to as Grandma opened the door and stepped in.

"Was just goin' to call ye, Grandma," Callie said. "Me and Josie has had a peck of fun. You know, it's a mite of comfort to have a woman around. I was tellin' Josie how lucky she is to have them two half-growed girls of hers." Callie was talking quickly, motioning to Josie, pushing Grandma to a chair facing the stove. Grandma smiled, for she had already seen the jars and sacks on the shelves. They thought she would fuss and refuse to take any gifts. Sure she would take them, and why not?

"My, my," she said, seating herself and looking over the table. "I ain't seen such good eatin' in a long time. I don't do much cookin' by myself; seems a bother when nobody's here but just me. Kind of a waste, though, all this stuff."

Josie laughed and passed the bowl of green beans. "This is a sort of a party, Grandma. Them beans looks as good to me as to you. Me and Sam didn't plant a second garden this year. Callie and Tom raised two crops of vegetables. Prettiest beets you ever saw and even some crooked-neck squash."

Grandma piled her plate full, her small eyes darting over the table. Green beans and potatoes, a large hunk of smoked bacon boiled with them, a bowl of yellow squash fried with onions, pickled beets, a loaf of corn lightbread, spiced plums, hard-boiled eggs cut up with fresh greens and greasy with bacon drippings. Not in years had Grandma seen so beautiful a table. A sense of thrift in her now made her wish to save, serve only a part of this meal.

"Did ye hear about what th' girls did with the gourds, Grandma?" Josie asked, her mouth full.

"What gourds?" Grandma hated talk at mealtime.

"Somebody give Tannie some strange gourd seeds last summer and she planted 'em along the fence. You never seen such purty things in your life! Long handles and striped in color. Tannie got some paint at th' store and made 'em every color you can think of. A picture in a mail-order catalogue give her the idee. Some folks drove by one day and seen them gourds dryin' on the porch and give her a dollar for two of 'em. Then Tannie rode over to the store with th' rest and sold the batch for five dollars."

"Mercy me!" Callie exclaimed. "Plain old gourds fer dippers. What did them folks want with 'em, anyhow?"

"One woman said she was going to hang hers up in the winder and put a vine in it."

"That ain't nothin'," Grandma said. "Back in the old days, folks on the mountain raised gourds as big as buckets. They used 'em to put stuff in like salt and sugar. I can remember when nobody had a tin bucket to their name."

"Good gracious, no buckets? What in th' world did they do without milk buckets?" Josie asked.

"I didn't say we didn't have no buckets," Grandma snapped. "I said tin buckets. We had pails made of red cedar and hickory. We had kegs the same and even barrels. We had copper pots and some pewter."

Grandma ate along quietly, pushing her food onto a spoon with a finger. It was so good and tasty she wished she could eat it in peace, have the time to fully savor it.

She picked up a piece of the corn lightbread, spread it thick with the fresh butter before her, butter she had not seen in so long. She looked over at Josie. Josie had aged considerably in the past year. There were streaks of gray in her black hair, long lines in her face. Her shoulders drooped from fatigue. Josie could not be more than thirty-five. She worked like a horse, letting them girls sit on the porch painting gourds!

"You young folks don't know what hard livin' is," Grandma said.

"It's hard enough," Josie said, sighing. "Sam has bought a farm with a good strong house and a well. There's even electric lights. I just can't wait to get in it. We can get ice every day and there's a hard road right by the house and a bus going by to take the kids to school."

"I wish you could see me and Tom's farm, Grandma," Callie said eagerly. "There's five acres in fruit and the river runs through the back fields. There's six rooms in that house, Grandma, and every one of them is papered on the wall with roses and vines in colors. And every room has two windows and the floors is smooth pine. I just can't wait to scrub and clean that house. Oh, I wish you could see it,

Granny. Reckon you might just come down for a visit once to see?"

Grandma listened to these accounts with mixed feelings. Life was over, her services would no longer be needed. If she had been essential to these neighbors, they would never go away from her. They wanted the valley and her, too. Grandma closed her eyes, remembering years of plenty. Perhaps never again would she see such a year.

"What you thinkin' about, Grandma?" Josie asked, eyeing her with pity.

Grandma opened her eyes and looked on Josie, resentfully. "I think plenty of things I don't tell nobody, Josie. Wouldn't do no good to tell you and Callie nothin', anyhow. All you can think about now is a house in the valley. A few years and I reckon you'll never look back and remember the land where ye was raised. Maybe it ain't your fault after all," she added, running a hand over her eyes. "Things has changed all along and been pointin' to this movin' and I'm th' only one who didn't know it. I'll have to get used to it."

"But you don't have to stay up here and get used to bein' by yourself," Callie told her.

"Nobody's been around tryin' to buy my land yet, Callie. Funny thing to me, everybody else seems to know all about this buyin' and what price to ask and what they're goin' to get."

"They ain't been to Bud Latham yet, either," Josie answered. "Sam says he allows it's on account of you and Bud having more land than the rest of the folks."

"You mean they might not want Grandma's land in the Park?" Callie asked, surprised.

80

Grandma laughed. "Wouldn't do 'em no good if they did want it. I ain't sellin' to nobody."

"Grandma, what would ye do if ye had a whole lot of money, say five thousand dollars? What would ye do, Grandma?" Josie leaned over the table, waiting for the answer.

Grandma grunted. "Seein' as I'll never own five thousand dollars, what need is there to figure on what I'd do with it?"

"But, supposin' th' Government allows you a price and lets you keep your place? That's what they're doin' all around."

Grandma pushed back from the table and rose to her feet. Dr. Mayberry had suggested something of the sort but she hadn't taken it in.

Callie explained further. "It seems you can get money for your place and live on it at the same time. Only thing, th' land belongs to th' Government and, after selling it, a person can't will it to nobody after he dies."

"Then, what in tarnation does a man like Sam want to take that money and throw it away on another place for? Why, that ain't good sense when he can have money fer his needs and work his farm just the same."

"And what about the young'uns when me and Sam dies, Grandma? Likely all that money would be gone by then, and them kids havin' to go live in a strange land where they won't know how to make a livin'. We figure on givin' 'em a start by leaving land to 'em in th' valley."

Grandma nodded. There was reason in this case, but it did not apply to Tom and Callie and she said as much.

"Dr. Mayberry says he wouldn't be surprised if me and

Tom didn't have a young'un by next summer, Grandma. He's goin' to give me a treatment."

Grandma stared at Callie. "You mean he's got some medicine that will make you have a baby? He beats all I ever seen, that valley doctor. I just don't understand him."

"He's a good man, Grandma. It's Dr. Mayberry's farm me and Tom is goin' to work in th' valley. Seems a person who goes around doctorin' folks is always doin' fer somebody else."

"Huh, a lot of good it does." Grandma reached for her cane and hobbled through her house, remembering the basket she had hidden in the bottom of the chest. She didn't want Josie and Callie to see it. She didn't want them to know she planned to trade her furniture to the doctor.

"Why didn't ye sun th' featherbed, too?" she called out.

"We was aimin' to." Callie and Josie walked in and approached the bed.

"Be careful," Grandma warned. "There might be a snake around."

"God a-mercy!" Callie stepped back and Josie and Grandma laughed.

"I remember in th' old days," Grandma said, "when a person had to shake th' covers ever' night for snakes. They was bad about gettin' in th' house. Once an old snake lived up in the rafters for years. Me and Ethan just left him alone. He killed the rats and kept other snakes away."

Callie sighed. "I'll be glad to be away from snakes, wild animals, and sich. Sometimes I ain't a bit sorry our old place burned down."

"You ought to be sorry about your furniture burnin'," Josie said. "It's just a sight about our old furniture,

Grandma. Some folks come by and Tannie and Jessie traded ever' bit of ours. You ought to see our stuff now. The girls spends half their time shining up them dressers with little mirrors on th' side. We got three shiny beds with springs and cotton mattresses."

"Who done th' tradin'?" Grandma asked.

"Why, some of them folks over to th' settlement. They had to sell out, too. They just swapped some of their stuff for ours. I can't understand what they want with that old furniture."

"There was a woman come to our house one day," Callie said. "Seems she wants to garner a lot of that old stuff to put in a house down in Gatlinburg, so everybody can stop by and look at it."

"What for?" Grandma asked.

"No tellin'," Josie answered. "Them valley folks has strange ways. I reckon it's goin' to be hard for me to fit in."

"You'll be so busy workin' and keepin' up with them girls, Josie, you won't have no time to worry over fittin' in," Grandma declared. "You better watch that Tannie! Remember what happened to Effie Tobin up on Knob Ridge? Them valley men just lay in wait fer girls like Tannie."

"What happened to Effie Tobin? I don't remember nothin' about her."

"It was back before your time, I reckon," Grandma continued. "Effie was the purtiest girl I ever seen and I reckon she was th' wildest. I don't mean she was bad, she was just like somethin' that growed wild in th' woods. Sometimes I think Effie was marked. She was born in a storm one night when Singing River was high and roaring in the hollow below th' house. Wouldn't be surprised if that river wasn't th' cause of everything. They say even now folks can hear Effie singing in th' woods. After what happened to her, Effie's ma moved to Pine Ridge and never did come back. She left Effie's baby and wouldn't even look at it. It was Polly Tobin who raised that girl child."

"Where was th' baby's pa?" Josie asked.

"That baby's pa was one of them valley men, Josie. He was a harp-playin' feller who must a-met Effie on the river. He hung around fer nearly a year and folks thought maybe he was goin' to marry Effie and Effie's ma was glad, hoping it would settle her down."

"You mean he got her in a fix and then run off and left her?" Callie asked.

"He got her in a fix all right but he didn't run off and leave her. Effie's twin brother, Eph, caught 'em in th' woods one day and Eph shot him dead right there on the spot."

"I reckon they caught Eph and put him in jail," Josie said.

"No such thing," Grandma said. "Back in them days, folks on th' mountain made their own laws. Eph was sorry he didn't make a weddin' after all, for Effie went as crazy as a bedbug after that. She wouldn't let that harp out of her hands and she played the saddest tunes you ever heard. She'd dance up and down the banks of that river, a-singing and a-playin'! Just let somebody come along and she'd start takin' off her clothes naked as a jaybird."

"Good gracious! What did they do with her?"

"Well, after her baby come she was worse, and one night she slipped out of the house, and next day they found Effie

84

drowned in the river."

"Did her baby live?" Callie asked.

"Last time I heard, it was livin'."

Callie leaned over. "Granny, I brought you my star quilt. I'll feel bad if you don't take it."

"Sure, I'll take it and be thankful, Callie. I'll think about ye when you're gone."

"And if I have a young'un next summer, you'll come down? Seems I don't trust Dr. Mayberry like I do you, Granny."

Granny smiled and looked off toward the mountains. "Yes, Callie, if I'm here next summer, I'll see to your young'un. But I wouldn't depend too much if I was you. The future ain't certain fer nobody anymore."

Grandma leaned back in her rocker, her eyes closing. Callie thought she slept, but Grandma did not sleep. There had come to her suddenly a vision, a strange picture that filled her sight and confused her mind. It was the face of a giant clock with long, reaching hands, hands that stood together and did not move. It was as if time was suspended. She might move those hands backward until they covered all the years she had known, but moving them forward was a gesture she couldn't make. Each day a second that failed to tick. A day would come when the hour would strike. What then? Death? Perhaps. Grandma opened her eyes and surveyed the rolling mist on the mountain peaks. Like a smoky veil it rose, disappearing heavenward.

"Oh, God of all my years, Thou knowest my end."

7

Two weeks passed and Dr. Mayberry had not returned. Each day Grandma tidied her house and sat on her porch to watch. Few people came along the cove road now. Occasionally, Aaron Biggers passed in his wagon but he didn't even look toward her house. Once Bud Latham rocked by in the saddle, calling out huskily as his horse passed the gate.

Grandma wondered about Bud. His acres were next to hers in size, but Bud had a family of young children and a young wife. He had children by his first wife, too. There had been rumors going around about the Lathams. It seemed Polly was bent on moving to the valley long before the law was passed about the land. Grandma reckoned Polly would be happy over this change. She couldn't picture old Bud off the mountain. How would he get his whiskey down there? It was killing him inch by inch, but nobody could tell him anything.

There was a feeling of frost in the air. One of these mornings she would wake up to hear rain on her roof, rain that would turn to sleet, and in no time winter would be upon her. Could she have misunderstood Dr. Mayberry? Suppose he didn't come after all? If she could only feel safe and settled. Those gifts Callie and Josie piled on her shelf filled a great need, but they would not last long. She must eat of this food sparingly until she knew how things stood with her.

After frost, she could go up on the ridge and gather walnuts and big acorns. Her tobacco was all gone and she missed not smoking, it made her more nervous. She wondered how it would feel to starve. Maybe it would be gradual and not hurtful after the first pangs of gnawing hunger. Maybe that was as good a way to die as any.

She got up and went to her lean-to, to take stock of her provisions. She wished she had some flour for biscuits. She hadn't had biscuits in so long and they would go so good with that sorghum.

"Hello, Grandma."

Grandma let out a squeal of fright and Dr. Mayberry patted her shoulder, apologizing.

"I thought you must have heard us coming. We made so much noise."

"I guess I'm gettin' deaf along with everything else, Doc. What did ye come fer?" Grandma looked into the doctor's face, hunting an answer she must find, not knowing her questions were written deep into the wrinkles that covered her own face.

"That depends on you, Grandma. Might be too big a

87

dose for you, I don't know. You been sleeping better?"

"Sure have. That's fine medicine you give me. Wish I had some more."

"I can fix that all right. Got a tooth doctor with me out on the porch. He's ready to yank 'em all out and make you some store teeth."

"You mean you ain't goin' to do it yourself?" Grandma was astonished.

Dr. Mayberry laughed and, taking Grandma's hand, he pulled her to the porch.

"This is Dr. Green, Grandma. He's a doctor that knows just one thing to cure and that's a fellow's teeth. He looks after mine and he can make you the prettiest set of false teeth you ever saw."

Grandma glanced at the young dentist and from him to the woman walking up the path. She was a pretty woman, but she was almost naked.

"Who is that?" Grandma asked, pointing.

"That's my wife, Mary, Grandma. Want you to meet her."

"Huh!" Grandma sniffed. "Why don't you put some clothes on when you git out? Ain't ye got no shame a-tall?"

Mary walked up the steps, laughing. "I've heard so much about you, Grandma. Heard about your furniture, too. You mind if I go in and see while the doctors look you over?"

Grandma had not expected all this. She had thought Dr. Mayberry would come about her teeth and about the furniture. Except for her needs, she would order them all out of her house. Her neighbors had forced her to this humiliation! To think that a long life should end in this fashion! Yes, it was going to end, so why should she worry so over preparations? That naked woman had walked right into her house without so much as by your leave; didn't even wait for an answer to her question. She was the one who wanted the furniture, not the doctor. Huh! She'd make her pay well for it; that is, if she decided to sell it. Grandma turned to Dr. Mayberry.

"When ye plannin' to pull them teeth?"

It was the dentist who spoke. "Suppose you sit here and let me examine your mouth, Grandma."

"Only six." She turned and spoke to Dr. Mayberry, who opened his case and took out a stethoscope.

"I'd like to examine your heart again if you don't mind, Grandma," he said.

"Go ahead," she answered, anxious to get it over.

"It won't hurt you a bit," the dentist said, awhile later. Grandma didn't believe that, but when all the teeth were out and she was spitting over the porch, she had to admit the wonders of the valley medicine and doctors. She asked so many questions and was so intrigued with the process of an impression of her gums being taken for the teeth; it was slow work.

"How long will it take before I get them teeth? How ye expect me to eat?"

Dr. Mayberry laughed. "You didn't have much to eat with anyway, Grandma. I'd say to eat mush and milk and soft-boiled eggs for a few days. I'll send the teeth up and it won't be long."

Milk and soft-boiled eggs, nothing. She could manage

the mush, for she had some meal on hand.

"How about lying down for a while?" the dentist suggested.

"What fer? I ain't sick. Ain't that woman in there messin' around my house? Go in there and see what she's doin', Doc."

"I have some medicine here I'd like for you to take right now," the dentist said.

"What's it fer?" Grandma asked.

"It will make your gums heal faster for one thing."

Grandma took the pill in her hand, weighing it. "It won't make me go to sleep, will it? I don't want to go to sleep. I got things to do."

The dentist smiled and reached for his pipe and tobacco tin. "No, it won't put you to sleep, Grandma. Like some tobacco?" he asked, seeing her eagerness. Grandma reached to her apron pocket and held out her pipe.

"I ain't had time to smoke all morning." Grandma leaned back in her rocker and, for the first time, glanced down the road. There was a large truck pulled back of the doctor's car and two men sat there, looking toward her house.

"What is all that?" she asked, pointing.

"You will have to ask Dr. Mayberry that question, Grandma," the dentist answered.

Grandma remembered then Dr. Mayberry's words: "Your furniture is worth a whole truckload of food." She got up and without excuse walked into her house. Dr. Mayberry was leaning against the mantel smoking a cigarette and Mary was examining the bed. Grandma stood there watching her out of eyes that were distrustful and calculating.

This was the first time Grandma had ever seen a modern woman of the valley. Dr. Mayberry was thinking, perhaps he should not have put so much on Grandma in one day. The effects of the novocaine would wear off presently and she would not feel so well. Perhaps she should not even be left by herself. If he could get that bed in and placed, and the food on her shelves, then give her a sedative. . . .

"Grandma." He walked over and took a chair close by. "You've known me for several visits now and you know I wouldn't take advantage of you in any way. I tell you again that your furniture is valuable, and sooner or later somebody is going to come up here and try to buy it."

"No Government feller has come about my land yet, Doc. Why you reckon they ain't been up here? They been to everybody else, exceptin' Bud Latham and my place. Tom Jenkins says they'll take your place away from you anyhow, and move you out. That ain't right, Doc. If I was a man, not an old woman. . . ."

Dr. Mayberry interrupted. "Have you any kinfolks to claim what you leave, Grandma?"

"Nobody but me. I was goin' to will my place to Tom Jenkins if he'd stayed on up here, but seems all th' folks around has turned against the land."

Dr. Mayberry considered words to explain the Park project, but he knew nothing he could say would offset the hurt of the people's disloyalty. It was this side Grandma saw, and it was the Government act that had brought it about.

"If this were my place," he said, "I'd not refuse to take money the Government offers. I'd take that money and buy some things I wanted, while I could use them. Darned if I'd die and let somebody else walk in and take what was due me, and that's what will happen, Grandma. If you die without a will, the Government will take over your place, bag and baggage."

"But that ain't right, Doc. You don't think it's right, do you?" Surely somebody agreed with her, Grandma thought. She could not have this feeling and be wrong entirely.

Dr. Mayberry was evasive. "Grandma, I'm just a plain healer like you. There are a lot of things in life that don't suit me, but I've found it best not to fight about them."

"I'm not goin' to move off th' mountain, Doc! Nobody can make me move!"

"I don't blame you, Grandma. But what about this? Suppose everybody in this cove does move to the valley, had you thought of what it will mean to be entirely alone up here?"

Grandma began to rock vigorously, unwilling to admit even to Dr. Mayberry that these very thoughts were bearing down upon her, keeping her awake at night.

"I been thinkin' to see Bud Latham. I don't believe Bud will move, not even if his wife is bent on th' valley. Bud ain't young like the rest. He's nearin' seventy." Grandma got up to spit in the fire, then she stood there looking over her cabin. "No," she said, firmly, "I ain't goin' to move, even if I'm up here by myself. I can't do nothin' but die and after I'm dead, bein' by myself won't make a bit of difference."

"And you'll agree to my bringing in that truckload of food and putting it on your shelves, setting up that nice bed, fixing up your house comfortably for winter?" The doctor spoke gently.

Grandma looked over at the cherry bed, the bed in which she had been born. Now that the time of giving up her things really had come, something tore at her heart, filling her chest with an emotion that was stifling. Yet she must make this trade, for only through it could she possibly retain her independence, stay with her home. It would not be the same home anymore, and when she closed her door against the night, she would turn and find herself in a strange atmosphere. Best not to think too much, just go on and get it over with. She felt tired and a little bit sick. If they would only hurry and leave her alone.

"All right, Doc," she said, "go on about bringin' in th' grub. I'll pile my quilts in a corner and empty them chest drawers."

This done, Grandma walked out to the back yard and seated herself on a box next the old cellar. She didn't want to see her things brought out of her front door. How many years? She tried to count on her fingers, then gave it up. Over a hundred years since that spool bed was placed in the corner for her mother. Queer, the old bed could be so costly.

And what would the mountain folks think when they came by and saw her things gone? She, who had fussed over the disloyalty of those who turned backs against old ways and customs, was doing that very thing herself now. But it had been forced upon her.

What was the world coming to if a person couldn't hold on to the house and land they rightfully owned, had lived on for over a hundred years? Who was back of this business, anyway? Well, whoever it was, when they came to her about her land, she'd deal with them! Fight in court! The law that took the land was the law of the courts, too.

She looked up when Dr. Mayberry and Mary stepped into the yard.

"Everything is all fixed now, Grandma. If you will tell me where the corn crib is, so I can get the other things."

Grandma pointed and Mary ran across the barn lot like a girl. Grandma followed her, distaste in her glance. Dr. Mayberry smiled. "Your gums hurting you yet, Grandma?" he asked, his voice kind.

Grandma got up and started toward her front porch, holding her long skirts with one hand and pecking her cane on the ground with the other. She made no answer to the doctor's question nor did she glance at the dentist on her porch. She hobbled up the steps into her cabin, then slammed the door behind her, setting the bar in place.

"Go on off, now!" she called out when Dr. Mayberry knocked. "You've done enough around here!"

"Take one of those pink pills and rest today, Grandma. Take another one in three hours. Don't take them any oftener than that. You understand me?"

"Of course, I ain't deef! Go on off now and let me alone!"

Grandma stood there feeling the soft carpet under her feet, a carpet covered with red roses. She laid her hand on the brass bed, a bed that shone like gold. She heard the car and truck moving down the cove road and then, all at once, it was quiet and she knew she was alone. She touched the red homespun coverlet of her mother's. They had left

94

her that.

Grandma reached for one of the pink pills and swallowed it dry. Then she turned and fell upon the new bed and to her surprise she sank deep into the softness of it, felt herself sway as she buried her head in the pillows. The silence of the log cabin was broken suddenly by a hysterical laugh that rose like a storm cloud crashing against the rafters. Then it came down mercifully in drops that wet her pillow in tears, bringing release, and finally, sleep.

8

BUD LATHAM straightened, let the hoe fall against his shoulder, then rubbed the small of his back with fingers that clutched here and there upon sore and stiffened places. He couldn't tell if it was the bones or just the flesh that was a-hurtin'. Bud reckoned he was just sore all over. His glance went up the straggling bean rows where weeds seemed to grow overnight. He no more weeded to the end of a row than they sprung up back at the beginning again. Planting a second crop of beans for the frost to get! Made him so consarned mad he didn't know what to do.

Pushing his hat to the back of his head, Bud leaned on the hoe and looked for the sun. Here and there, patches of sunshine pushed through the clouds, clouds that hung low, massing in great billows, pressing toward the earth, and hiding the tips of the Chimneys.

Rain, he told himself. Well, he didn't care if it did rain.

He wished to Gawd it would rain for a week without stopping. His back would hurt worse on account of it but he could rest without feeling of guilt. There were times when he resented this new conscience of his, regretted the promises he had made. He resented most that preacher a-shoutin' and a-cryin' over him, pulling from Bud feelings he didn't know he had, exacting promises no man in his right mind would have made. Trouble was, every time he tried to break loose, every time he was on the edge of forgetting, lapsing back to his former ways of living, there came a prick of remembrance that was a pain.

Sometimes in the night Bud had visions. Arms beckoned to him. He found himself rising to keep apace, running to find what was just a light, seeking what he couldn't find and with it all, waking up of a morning as tired as a feller plowing corn all day.

Bud watched the clouds gather and bunch, then fall to one side and shadow the whole mountainside. He looked down to the valley and marked the patches of color here and there, saw cloud shadows move from one green patch to another like a monster creeping up silently. Spitting on his hands, he rubbed them together and started in once more with the hoe. No fool like an old fool, he told himself. Marryin' an eighteen-year-old girl, and him an old man with growed children. No wonder folks laughed at him years back. No wonder young Bud run off and left all the work for him to do. Susie run off, too, and married one of them Pratts; selling whiskey and making money hand over fist for all Bud never saw no help from Susie. Oh, they'd give him whiskey if he went over for it but Bud couldn't have whiskey any more. He'd promised that

97

preacher he'd not touch another drop, so help him Gawd, and if it hadn't been for the Gawd part, he'd pay no attention to none of it.

Looking down the hollow, Bud saw smoke curl up from the washing fire. Polly had got him out before he'd swallered his vittles, gathering wood. Dad-burned luck of his! Married a woman so all-fired full of energy she made him tired just to look at her. Always a-doin' something, never could set still. Life wasn't meant to be lived this way. Polly was raisin' them kids to do nothing but read books, said a little larnin' was needed so they could do more than live like hogs. Well, he wasn't goin' to put up with it another day. Polly had them kids in a school down in the valley now, and so far as he was concerned she could go down there, too. Reaching the end of the bean row, he walked over to lean on the rail fence, watching Tom Jenkins trottin' his mules down the road.

"Hey there, Tom. Light and hitch fer a spell."

"Ain't got much time, Bud," Tom answered, bringing the mules to a stop. "Fine crop of beans there, but I bet the frost gets 'em."

"Hope to Gawd it does." Bud took out a plug of tobacco, bit off a chew.

"You don't need all them beans, do you?" Tom asked.

"Hell, no! Got the corncrib full now. It's Pol, wantin' to get money to buy shoes fer them kids of hers. Say, Tom, you movin' to th' valley like all th' rest?"

"Yep, we're moving in three weeks. Goin' to work Doc Mayberry's farm; best land I ever seen, Bud. Now it's all settled, I don't feel happy about it somehow. Kinder miss things up here. Sam Acree says down in th' valley a feller has to work all th' time to keep things going, and there ain't no huntin' down there, neither. A feller has to buy a license to own a gun and then when ye get a license you ain't got no place to hunt."

"Is it so about 'em givin' money for th' land and lettin' ye live on your place just th' same?" Bud asked.

"That's what they offered me."

"Then what are you and Callie movin' fer? You ain't got no kids to worry over and save fer."

"That's goin' to be changed, Bud. Doc Mayberry says ain't no reason why Callie can't have young 'uns. He's goin' to fix it fer us."

"Good Gawd! Don't know what in tarnation ye want with a trifling family, Tom, nothin' but work and nobody satisfied with nothin' ye do. Gawd meant for ye to have kids he'd a sent 'em to ye natural. I don't hold with that furrin doctorin'."

Tom smiled. "I reckon you've had too many young uns, Bud. You don't know how lonesome a house is without kids. You ain't got nothin' to work for that way. And it's awful hard on a woman."

"Well, so far as I'm concerned, you young fellers can have th' valley. I ain't movin' down there."

Bud had been traveling toward these words so long, it seemed he had said them before. Now that he had said them, the decision became a fact, one he would stand back of and no matter what happened.

Tom sat there regarding Bud, thinking about Grandma Weller. If Bud was in any way dependable, to know he was staying with the mountain would bring relief to Tom about Grandma. He considered talking it over with Bud when a voice echoed from the hollow—

"Bu-ud!" Bud spat over the fence and settled his elbows comfortably on the rails.

"Ain't that Polly callin' ye?" Tom asked.

"Wouldn't be surprised if it ain't." Bud spat again.

"I reckon she wants something." Tom suggested.

Bud didn't say anything.

"Well, I got to be goin'." Tom lifted the reins and called to his mules. "You better see them Government fellers about stayin' up here if Polly gets the money and moves off."

Go see them Government fellers? Hell, let them come up here if they had any dealings with him. He wouldn't ask 'em about stayin' up here, either. He'd just stay. And if he didn't need money so Polly could take them kids to th' valley, then he wouldn't even sell his land. Nobody could drive him out of the mountains. He could look after himself, too. Yes, and damn if he hadn't better start thinking of ways of doing it. Winter come sudden in th' mountains.

Bud looked up to see Polly plodding up the slope, the baby on her hip, three-year-old Sammy tagging in the rear.

"Bud," she called, "is dinner ready yet?"

"How in hell do I know if it's ready? Ye think I'm goin' to petticoat round a stove and put reins on a kettle?"

Bud lifted the hoe to his shoulder and passed Polly, making for the house. Reaching the porch, he dropped the hoe and settled himself in a straight chair tilted against the wall. Wouldn't be long now before he could do more resting than working. No need to try napping now. Polly was swelled close on to bustin'! He had slashed things on the surface for days now and the whole business was going to come to a head. He dreaded it, but best to settle it once and for all. He pulled his hat over his eyes and went on thinking.

Now that this Government money would offset his obligations to Polly and the kids and not hurt his conscience none, well, it was like a gift from God. Bud never had paid any attention to Grandma Weller saying his rheumatiz came from drinking. And what if it did? Grandma had some tonic to do away with it, didn't she? Grandma! Tom Jenkins was on the way now to Grandma's. Him and Callie was goin' to take her with them to the valley. Gawd A'mighty! He couldn't let Grandma Weller go out of his range! The very thought was fear and desperation.

Polly seated herself on the porch and opened her bosom to let the baby suck. Whimpering and clutching at her skin, nudging like a calf, young Clem found himself the recipient of Polly's pent-up anger at Bud. She pulled the baby from her breast and administered a sound smack. The resulting scream brought a wince to Bud's face and he tried to shut out of his consciousness the uproar with which he seemed to be constantly surrounded.

"Put that young 'un down and give him a piece of cornbread. What ye reckon Gawd give him them teeth for, if not to chew on something?" he bellowed.

Polly dropped Clem to the floor, where his cries rose louder and more wrathful. "Look here, Bud Latham," she shouted. "I've had all I can stand of your good-for-nothin' ways. If you don't brace up when we get to the valley, I ain't goin' to put up with ye another five minutes. Ye hear me?"

"So!"

Bud settled back in his chair and eyed Polly reflectively. "You ain't goin' to put up with me, eh? How about me doin' a little puttin' up, too? So fer as I can see, Polly, you've already moved to th' valley. You can't stay away from that school long enough to cook me a decent mess of vittles. Well, you might as well know right now. I ain't movin' to th' valley a-tall. But you can go, and anytime that suits ye."

Polly lifted the baby to her lap and sat back, unprepared for this turn of events. She was Bud's wife. Such being so, he was boss of his land in the eyes of the Government folks. They'd do what he said. For all her twelve years of married life, Polly had never been able to get an acknowledgment from Bud that all this was half hers. He even said, "them kids of yourn," just like he didn't have nothin' to do with it.

Living from day to day wasn't enough for Polly. She was forever trying to show Bud that to raise a surplus and pile up something for the future was necessary, not only for the children but for old age that was fast coming to him. When the Government came in and offered money for the land, it just didn't seem possible. She spent weeks trying to understand it, then she went down to the school in Gatlinburg and asked questions but the answers she got seemed very silly to her.

A sound from Bud drew Polly's attention. How in the world could he set hisself down in broad daylight and sleep like a hog? Tobacco juice dribbled from his mustache, coarse and bristly, yellow and unkempt. His mouth opened and closed with accompanying sounds like a pig's grunt. His eyes were sunk into his head like the stem end of a pumpkin vine, his skin yellow and leathery. His teeth were stumps, broken off here and there to the gums. His whiskers stood out straight and bristly.

Polly's gaze took in the full length of Bud's slouched figure: pants lapped over at the waist and held together with a safety pin. The shirt, once blue, was devoid of any color, unless the face of the earth had color. One sleeve was entirely gone and easily accounted for on the handle of the hoe, wrapped round and round to offset blistered hands. His brogans were laced together with twine, and one was hanging loose and dangling around his bare and dirt-crusted ankle.

The picture was that of a skeleton assuming a grotesque masquerade, a pose of restfulness while achieving the opposite: indifference and complete dejection.

Polly's contact with the people in the valley school had influenced her more than she knew. She looked back now and remembered that her father had said this was a good marriage, what with Bud owning such a good place and being old and uncertain in years. Polly sniffed, and reflected there was nothing uncertain about Bud. For all he was as yellow as a pumpkin, stiff and sore with rheumatiz and wrinkled as a summer squash, he'd live on years like Grandma Weller.

A gust of wind swept down the road, bringing with it a tall spiral of dust, a whirlwind that seemed to stop in front of the house and spread itself over the yard and onto the porch. Sammy cried out, wiping sand from his eyes.

"Wake up, Bud!" Polly jerked at his sleeve while slipping the now-wakeful Clem to his feet by a chair. "Look to th' valley, Bud. Nothin' but clouds, can't see a thing. Fog's comin' up and it's gettin' cooler. Better hunt th' cow and get the milkin' over. Sammy! Stop that bawlin' and look after Clem while I go for the clothes."

Three-year-old Sammy crawled up the steps, whining. "Ma, I'm hungry."

"All right, honey. I'll get ye some corn bread. Don't let Clem put nothin' in his mouth."

Bud rose and shook himself, betting his bottom dollar that infernal cow had wandered halfway to Grandma Weller's. Thirty minutes later, he slipped from the hill down into the roadway still calling, "Sook-cow, sook-cow."

The fog had settled like a blanket over the mountain, clinging to the trees, clutching at the earth, spreading a dampness that was equal to a shower of rain. It wet deep into Bud's scant clothing, stood in drops on his bushy eyebrows, then rolled down his face to be lost in a mass of tangled whiskers. He shivered and blew out his breath in great gusts, swearing loud. Stumbling on, he called out again, "Sook-cow . . . sook-cow," afraid to go back home without the cow and wishing to Gawd he didn't own a cow in the first place to pin him to duty.

Approaching Grandma's place, he looked up the pathway where her cabin seemed larger in the shadows, where the smoke rising from more than usual fire pushed at the fog and hugged the earth around the chimney. Leaning on the gate, his attention was attracted by a noise close to the back steps. The sound was unmistakable. He slipped furtively to the cabin and, peeping around the corner, he viewed what to anybody else on the mountain was a low-down and ornery sight, dishonest and unexplainable. Squatting on an upturned lard can, Grandma was talking in low tones to Bud's cow and all the time milking with two hands streams of milk into a two-gallon bucket.

Bud was so filled with humor, so tight with laughter, he could hardly hold himself in. Pore old Granny! Dad burn the luck! Grandma could have th' cow if she wanted her. He would give Grandma anything he had if she would just stay up on the mountain and not go to the valley with Tom and Callie. An idea came to him, a plan. He peeped around the corner again and watched Grandma shoo the cow away, then walk into her lean-to and close the door behind her. With more haste than anybody had seen manifested in years, Bud slipped through the fog after his cow and turned her toward Grandma's rickety barn. Driving her in, he closed and barred the door, then he sat down to wait a decent interval.

Darkness had come now with the fog and, sitting with his back against the barn door, Bud shivered, rubbed his aching hip, and kept his eyes on the point of light from the lean-to. He had heard some tales from Jed Simmons and Aaron Biggers about Grandma garnering pay for her doctorin'. They were spreading it around like it was a crime, tellin' folks what to expect. Hell! Why shouldn't Grandma get something for what she did? How else was she to live? Grandma had brought every one of Polly's kids and, so far as he knew, Polly had never given her a thing. Bud decided now upon a course of action. When the light moved from the lean-to to the cabin, he knew Grandma was through with her supper, so he gathered himself together and made for the house.

"Who is that, anyhow?" Grandma called out.

Bud had lifted the latch and was surprised to find the

door held fast against him. He had never known Grandma to bar her door. That meant she was afraid.

"It's me, Grandma, Bud." There was a scraping sound as the bar was lifted, then the light from the oil lamp in Grandma's hand shone full in Bud's face.

"Well, you sick or something?" Grandma was tickled to see Bud. She had been wondering how all this moving struck him. She set the lamp on the table and seated herself before the fire.

"Pull up a chair and set," she said. "Kinder lonesome tonight with the heavy fog." Grandma took her pipe from her apron pocket, filled it from a tobacco tin, then reached to the hearth for a coal.

Bud stood there before the fire, warmth creeping through his chilled bones. Nights were getting colder now. Winter was not far off.

"Wish I had me a quart o' whiskey," he said, looking toward Grandma, hopefully.

"Humph! Whiskey ain't what you need, Bud." Grandma lifted her pipe from her mouth and pushed at the tobacco with a forefinger.

Bud looked up interested. "What do I need then?" he asked.

"I reckon a tub of hot water and soapsuds would be th' best thing fer ye right now. You smell like a line of wet didies. All old men smell like pee."

Bud bristled. "Now, you look a-here, Grandma Weller. Just because you're gettin' old don't mean ye can say hurtin' things to folks. Maybe Jed and Aaron is right. You are gettin' too bossy."

"I ain't a bit consarned over Jed and Aaron. You talk

too much anyhow, Bud Latham. Reach that cob pipe on the mantel and I'll give ye a bit of tobaccy, the like of which you never tasted afore."

"I reckon something to eat would do me more good, Grandma. I ain't et a bite since mornin'. Howsomever, I don't reckon ye have any milk around and that's all my stummick will stand these days."

Grandma didn't bat an eyelash over Bud's thrust. She didn't falter in her rocking and her pipe puffed just as evenly as before. Why, she was a regular old possum, Bud thought.

"Yep, I can give ye some milk, Bud. I don't reckon ye could tell a mite o' difference in it from what you've been drinkin' either."

Grandma walked to the lean-to and came back with a pint jar of milk, a plate of turnips, and a couple of corn pones. She put these in Bud's hands, then sat down to resume her rocking and smoking, looking all the time into the fire, paying no mind whatever to Bud. He watched her as he ate the food and decided he hadn't tasted such cooking since his mother's day. Sopping up the last bit with a piece of bread, he set the dishes on the floor and leaned back in his chair.

"Grandma, ain't no use you tryin' to hide things. I seen ye a-milkin' old Bess awhile back."

Grandma continued to look in the fire. "Wouldn't be surprised if ye didn't. I milked her right out in th' open where anybody could a-seen if they was of a mind to. When folks lets their cows wander over people's land, trample down their herb gardens and over their flowers, they ain't got no complaints. I'd a-shut that cow up in my barn and milked her a whole week if I could a-got her in there." Granny reached in her pocket for the tobacco tin and handed it to Bud.

"Don't ye go to talkin' of me bein' old. I may be old enough to be yore ma, but I can look after myself a sight better than you can right now. What's this I hear about Pol going to th' valley and leaving you up here?"

Bud brought his chair to all four legs and half rose in anger. "So that's what folks is saying! Tom Jenkins told it, I reckon. Well, it's so about me not goin' to th' valley. I told Polly she could go when she got good and ready, but it's not her leaving me, it's me that ain't going. I'm staying' 'cause I want to, and Polly ain't got nothin' to do with it." Bud spat in the fire and puffed vigorously on the cob pipe. Grandma turned her eyes on him.

"Them Government fellers tell ye to stay here?" she asked.

"Gawd A'mighty, Grandma! What's that got to do with me livin' on my own land? This is a free country, ain't it? I got a deed to my place. I got two deeds, one's from old No'th Ca'lina and one's from Tennessee. I reckon that's proof enough it's mine."

"I got two deeds too, Bud, but Doc Mayberry says that don't make a bit of difference if the Government decides it wants my place. Tom Jenkins says you balk at moving and they'll bring th' Army over here." Grandma settled back in her rocker and eyed the fire, dreamily.

"I'd sort o' like to see a Army," she added.

Bud leaned forward to put his question, fearful of the answer. "Are you going to th' valley with Tom and Callie, Grandma?"

Grandma turned to look at Bud, wondering if it was possible for him to change, be dependable. If he really was going to stay on the mountain, it was a great relief to know she would not be entirely alone. But, if Bud was to carry on his drinking, then he would be dependent on her and she might be in a worse fix than by herself.

"No," she said, firmly, "I ain't goin' to th' valley with nobody. I'm stayin' in my own house and th' Government or nobody else can make me move."

"That shore is good news, Granny. I'm goin' to stay, too, but I don't mind you knowin' that being by myself up here don't suit me. I reckon everybody else will go, exceptin' us. Don't you worry none, Granny. I'll look after ye."

Grandma smiled. The idea of Bud looking after anybody was funny. And where would he get whiskey when the Pratts moved off? Maybe if he went without liquor for a few months, he'd change. Anyway, drunk or sober, it was better to have Bud around than nobody at all.

Bud rose and glanced over the cabin. For the first time he noted a change and his eyes opened wide.

"What in tarnation has happened around here, Grandma? Don't look natural."

Grandma smiled. "I been doin' a little tradin' with Doc Mayberry." When Grandma smiled, Bud got a shock that set him back in his chair.

"Yore teeth, Grandma!" he gasped. "Where's yore old teeth?"

"Doc Mayberry brought a feller up here from th' valley who pulled 'em out, then he made me these new teeth and sent 'em up by Tom Jenkins. Doc says it won't be long afore I won't have no pains in my shoulders. He's a fine feller, that Dr. Mayberry." Grandma got up and motioned Bud to the lean-to.

Bud stood there completely overcome by what he saw. Shelves were piled high with canned goods and barrels, and boxes stood around the wall. Why, it looks like a store, he thought. Grandma didn't need him to look after her, not with all that winter provender. Bud's spirit fell, and he walked back and slumped into a chair by the fire.

Outside, the wind was rising. He could hear the old gate knocking against the barn-lot fence. From the hollow below the house, the wind moaned and echoed through the cove. Gawd, this house of Grandma's was a lonesome place. Seemed like she would dread winter all by herself up here. He remembered, then, the barred door and he knew Grandma was afraid, whether she would admit it or not.

"Grandma," he said gently. "I didn't know ye had all this. I didn't even know if ye meant to stay up here. I come over thinkin' maybe I could be of as much help to you as you could be fer me, but seems you don't need no help from anybody. All th' same, that cow of mine is in your barn and she can stay out there. Gawd knows I owe ye more than a cow fer all you've done fer us."

"What'll Polly say about that cow?" Grandma asked, delighted with the gift.

"Don't make me no difference what she says. She'll take up with that school in th' valley and, likely as not, get a job with weaving quilts, not even wait fer th' Government to pay up. I hope to Gawd she does." Bud got up and made ready to leave. He stood waiting for her to speak, unable to press his need of her further in the face of her prosperity.

"I wouldn't tell nobody but you, Bud, but I don't hanker to stay by myself up here. Be a mite of comfort, knowin' somebody is over th' hill, comin' by ever' now and then."

Grandma wouldn't allow herself to build up hope about Bud Latham. Time would tell and nothing else. Let them Government fellers come along and lay money in Bud's lap, and no telling what he'd do. Bud meant well, but he wasn't the dependable kind.

"I'd better be goin'," he said. "I'll come over tomorrow and fix th' rails on that barn-lot fence so's the cow can't run off."

"If ye mean it about me having th' cow, I'm right proud, Bud. I miss not gettin' milk."

Bud slipped out into the night and Grandma adjusted the bar on the door and made ready for bed. It was the prettiest bed she ever saw. Every morning she shined the brass so it looked like gold. That mattress was so soft and thick it made a body feel like they were resting on feathery clouds. She covered her fire with ashes, then crawled into the brass bed with a long and contented sigh.

9

Tom Jenkins stood on Grandma's porch holding a hammer and a saw. "Well, Granny, that fixed your house some better, but I wish I had some new shingles for the roof. I'm afraid them old ones won't hold out th' winter."

"Don't ye worry, Tom. I'm proud ye done this much. Don't know how I'm goin' to pay ye, though."

"Grandma, you're always talking of neighbors and yet you won't let nobody do anything for you."

Grandma got up and walked over to the step, seating herself beside Tom. "When I reached the place where I didn't have nothing to exchange for kindliness, Tom, when I got so old I couldn't even depend for certain on my own self, then it made me beholdin' to you and Callie and anybody else who wanted to do for me. I never thought of such things till I found myself old of a sudden. Seems now you're right about providin' for a future. Seems Polly is right, too, and Bud Latham is a fool not to appreciate Polly. Trouble is, I ain't got anything to exchange any more and no way of gettin' anything."

Tom knocked his pipe against a post and blew through the stem. "You forget you got money in your place here, Grandma. Don't see to save my life why a sensible person would set out to fight th' government and go to law. Why, a man can get th' money and live on up here just the same, if he wants to. I can't see no argument anywhere."

"Is that Lige Holder really goin' to law over his land?"

"Yep. Dr. Mayberry told me about it. It sure is mixed up and I feel sorry for the Government men."

"Why?"

"Well, it seems some slickers in the valley heard about makin' the Park even before we knew it up here, so some of 'em bought up a lot of the farms before the Government men got around.'"

"What did they want to do that for?"

"Oh, that's to show how slick them valley men are, Grandma. They was plannin' to buy the land cheap and then hold up the Government fer a big price when they come around to buy."

"And beatin' th' mountain folks out of that money!" Grandma stormed.

"Nobody can beat th' Government, Grandma. They know what they're doing. Doc Mayberry said one valley feller paid three thousand for a farm up here and the Government wouldn't give him but twenty-five hundred. That means he lost five hundred on the trade. He went to court about it but it didn't do him no good."

"I guess I know how Lige Holder feels about his land,

Tom. Is he an old feller?"

"Lige has been tryin' to sell his land for ten years. Nobody wanted to buy it 'cause the timber on it is in such places you can't get it out."

"Is that a fact!" Grandma exclaimed. "You mean if timber on your land is so ye can get it out, then the land is worth more money?"

"Sure, Grandma. When they appraise your land, they give ye credit fer everything. As fer that old fool of a Lige, I'll bet he never saw a thousand dollars in his life, let alone ten thousand."

"Ten thousand dollars!" Grandma shouted. "You mean to tell me a feller asked th' Government that much money fer his land?"

"The Government decides the worth of the land, Grandma, then they make th' offer. They offered Lige ten thousand fer his place but he's holding out for fifteen thousand. It's all on account of them men from th' valley who bought land up here! They are mad, and stirrin' men like Lige to cause trouble. Now Lige has got a lawyer to fight for his rights and he ain't got enough sense to know that lawyer will get th' biggest slice of that land money. Doc Mayberry said everybody in th' valley was a laughin' about it. There's been three or four cases in court already. I wouldn't want to make myself a laughin' stock."

"So them Government fellers makes th' price, eh? Don't ask what you think or want!" This was something Grandma needed to know, so she would be prepared when the agents came to see her.

Tom laughed. "Well, Grandma, you'd better join forces with Lige Holder since you seem to have the same ideas."

Grandma disregarded that remark. "Listen, Tom, what ye think my place is worth? How will I know if it's a good and fair price? This house ain't much, but it's my home and I wouldn't trade it for two of them houses in th' settlement. I got a thousand acres, Tom."

Tom turned to look Grandma in the eye. "So you're going to be sensible and not fight about it. Is that it?"

Grandma sniffed. "I didn't say no such thing! Anyhow, maybe they won't even want my land in that Park! That's what Josie said."

"Oh yes, they will. They'll come around most any time now. Just think of havin' a lot of money to buy things you never had."

"But I don't want to be beat out of a rightful price, Tom. You heard anything about th' Biggers? How is Aaron taking all this?" she asked.

"He's listening to that Lige Holder, and I believe Aaron's a little scared."

"Scared of what?" she asked.

"All that big family of girl children and takin' 'em off to a strange country. It's bad enough him losing his mill trade with folks movin' off. It was right handy to take your corn over to Aaron and get it ground to meal."

"You mean they already been to Aaron and set a price on his place?" Grandma asked, surprised.

"No, I don't think they have yet. Your land, Bud's and Aaron's is the last in the cove."

"You mean they already give you th' money fer your place, Tom?"

"It'll be along most any time, Grandma. Doc Mayberry said a feller didn't have to worry over th' Government.

Where's your papers, Granny?"

Grandma's eyes lit up with excitement and she motioned Tom to her cabin. He watched while she knelt and lifted a floor board.

"Good Gawd! Ain't you got no better place than that? It's a wonder th' rats ain't et up them papers."

Grandma sniffed. "That's where Pa kept 'em. He sawed that log and boarded up that hole. Nobody would ever think to look in such a place fer valuables, and I ain't got no rats in my house!"

"I don't know how you do it. We even have flyin' squirrels around our place. The way they make nests is a sight." Tom sat on the floor beside Grandma and watched while she spread the yellowed papers before him.

"There's two deeds," she said, proudly. "This here is from No'th Ca'lina, and this is from Tennessee. I reckon nobody could question it's my land."

Tom picked up the Tennessee deed and began to spell out words. " 'Bound on the north by twin poplar trees, running due west—' why, Granny, this deed shows your land overlaps Bud Latham's, and derned if here ain't a slice out of the Biggers place, too!"

Grandma stared at Tom, half rising from the floor. "What's that? You mean to tell me Aaron Biggers and Bud Latham is claimin' part of my land?"

Tom laughed and pushed Grandma back to the floor. "Don't get riled now, Granny. Them Government fellers knows how to fix this. They said half the land deeds up here showed overlapping. They've got records in th' courthouse and if any fussing takes place, they do the settling and whether you sold your land or not. Best be friends with 'em. Goin' against th' Government is like battin' your head against a mountain. When the Government decides to do something, it does it."

"Huh." Grandma grunted. "Seems like they didn't have no trouble movin' some of you fellers out. I can't understand this Park business, to save my life. What is a park, anyhow, Tom?"

Tom rubbed his eyes wearily, then rose and stretched. "Grandma, Doc said the Government decided it wasn't right for just a few folks to see all the wonders of these mountains. He said there wasn't any other mountains like these in the world. So the Government decided to own it all and let anybody come in that wanted to, and come free. That means a park."

"You mean folks can just drive up here and walk in my house any time it suits 'em? Whoever heard of sich a thing? I just wish they'd try it." Grandma got up and walked toward her kitchen. "Sit on th' porch a minute, Tom, I got something to send Callie."

Tom walked to the gate and looked down the hollow and to the Chimney Tops beyond. He took in the hillside acres back of the cabin, acres full with stubble, untended for years. Small trees were growing, the whole place going slowly back to woods. On that ridge up there were trees that had seen no axe or saw for a hundred years.

A thousand acres! he mused. Why, Grandma had more land than he knew. She would get a big price for her place. She above all others should not have been left to the last.

Dr. Mayberry had said the state money had run out and the Government was now taking over. It would take a few months, he'd said, then there would be plenty of money to buy the rest of the Park land. Some land was bound to be left for Government and not state purchase. Tom did not understand all this but he felt sure it was fair. Only thing was, it seemed hard that Grandma was left to the last. He looked up now as she came to the porch.

"Tom," she said, "Callie might not get over here again. I want to give her some medicine and tonics. When ye get to the valley and change drinkin' water, ye might get a spell of liver. Th' cure for it is in this brown bottle. Here's a box of curin' salve for sores and th' like. Here's a build-up tonic to take in th' spring and here's some cough tonic Callie lays store by. And if one of ye gets with a cold, rub this on your chest; warm it first and cover up with a flannel rag." Grandma laid the box on the step and Tom reached for it gratefully.

"That sure is a fine present, Grandma, I don't know how me and Callie . . ." Tom's voice broke as he looked at Grandma.

"Ah, honey," Grandma reached over and pulled Tom's head to her breast. "You've been like a grandson to me, Tom."

"You said my leaving th' mountain was good riddance. I been thinking about that."

Grandma pushed him away and walked down into the yard. "Well, don't think about it any more, 'cause it ain't so. The way things is happening around here, I change my mind every day. Looks like a person can't hold to any sense a-tall."

Tom walked toward his wagon and when he reached the gate, he turned and called back, "Grandma, if I was you, I wouldn't take less than ten thousand dollars for my place.

But let them make an offer first, they might give more."

Grandma stood in the yard until Tom's wagon disappeared around a curve in the cove road. Ten thousand dollars! Oh, no. He could not have meant that much. Grandma had never owned two hundred dollars in her life. She remembered what Dr. Mayberry had said: "The Government will take your land, anyway, so why not use that money for things you want?"

Grandma looked at her cabin. When she was gone, they would likely tear her house down. Dr. Mayberry was right. If she died without a will, the Government might walk right in and take possession. Well, they were going to have to pay her for it, and a price she set on the land herself! She wished the Government fellers would come on. It was getting colder every day now. She walked up her steps thinking of what she would buy when her money came. She would get a brand-new kitchen stove, and a new set of dishes with roses on the plates.

10

HOMER SIMMONS shifted his weight, swung one leg over the side, and made no objection when the mule came to a full stop in the river.

"Drink, ye bony critter. You won't be tastin' water as cold and fine as this in th' valley."

The mule lifted its head, its ears extended, listening.

"Nothing but th' falls a-roaring. Don't get het up now." Homer dug his bare toes in the mule's flanks and urged it up the bank. Jumping to the ground, he tied the rope rein to a sapling and turned back to the river.

Ain't more than ten o'clock, he said to himself. A body would think different, it's so dark and shadowed here in the hollow.

From his pocket Homer took a piece of lye soap and, after glancing up and around, he satisfied himself as to his privacy and pulled off his clothes. He stood waist-deep in the river, the water swirling fast and cold against him. Twenty yards below, the river widened to a deep pool and he cursed under his breath when a trout leaped from the current, sending wide ripples against the mossy bank.

"Gawd A'mighty! Three pounds or more," he exclaimed. Homer wished he had his rifle. He had hidden it under the floor back at the house. He felt in the pockets of his overalls and took out a ball of cord and a hook. Well, why not? If his father come home of a sudden and found him gone, he'd beat him whether he was off an hour or all day. Pa would whale hell out of him anyhow if he knew them sacks of Irish 'taters was on the way to Grandma Weller's.

Seating himself on a rock at the edge of the water, he made a quick lather and began to scrub himself vigorously. He dipped his head and covered his long hair with the suds, bent upon removing a little dirt before seeing Grandma.

"Gawd! The water's like ice, and I ain't had time fer a wash all summer," he muttered, shivering. Homer's glance went up the riverbank to his shirt and overalls, so dirty and ragged he loathed putting them on again, clean as he now was.

I'll wash them, too, he decided, and while they're dryin', I'll take me a try at that fish.

Soaking his two garments, he wadded them into a ball, rubbed in lye soap, sousing his clothes ever' so often in the river. He spread-eagled his overalls on a rock, hung his shirt on a laurel bush, and turned his attention to the fish.

Walking along the river's edge, he lifted stone after stone, looking for crayfish. He wished he had some chicken guts. They made fine bait. Gee, it was peaceful down here in th' hollow. Homer walked up the slope, then turned to look back. He could not see the river now for the dense thicket, but he could hear it. The roar of the falls filled the hollow with musical sounds. He hugged the moment to him, feeling a happiness and satisfaction, a kinship that made of the woods and himself all one big and surrounding world. Why couldn't a feller measure his working days so that all life wasn't pushed, full to the brim with plowing? When crops were laid by, came woodcutting, butchering of the hogs, caring for the stock. It seemed work was never done, and it shouldn't be that way.

Squirrels were gathering nuts for winter. Homer smiled, seeing a gray tail flying up a tree trunk. There were lots of nuts this year and that meant a hard winter. Homer had heard Grandma say when nuts were plentiful and when the corn was heavy with shucks, it meant winter would ride in like a lion and roar on the mountain. Coming out in the open glade lush with grass, he caught a grasshopper and returned to the river.

After that, time was immaterial to Homer. He dreamed away there on the river, naked as the day he was born. He stretched, belly down, on a flat rock that hung over the deep pool. His mind went back to his home. There had been two hard days of work, getting things together for moving to the valley. Jed got him out of bed before daylight to hunt the hogs in the woods. Gathering the corn had been a rushed job. If his father had helped with the work instead of waving a hickory limb even to the little kids, the work wouldn't have been so hard.

The thought of moving to the valley filled Homer with

a great unhappiness, even foreboding. If it wasn't for his mother, he'd not even go back. He'd start running and wouldn't stop until he reached some far place in the mountains where Jed couldn't find him. Well, some day he'd be old enough to decide things for himself and what he would decide would not be living in the valley.

Homer had forgotten the fish when a tug almost slipped the line from his hand.

"Gawd!" He jerked the cord, held tight, and laughed as the trout leaped from the water and back again, churning and circling, tugging and fighting to get free.

"I've got ye, old feller. No need to fuss and fume. Keep on wearing yourself down." Homer threw his head back and roared with laughter and happiness, his voice echoing up the hollow.

When he lifted the fish from the water a few minutes later, he sat down in awe and wonderment. Never had he seen so big a trout caught in the mountains. He was so downright proud he wished he could take it over to the settlement store and show it around. Shucks! He didn't have no more freedom than a mule. Looking up through the trees, Homer noted the position of the sun, and groaned. Jed would be home by now and he'd whale hell out of him. There were those two sacks of potatoes to deliver to Grandma Weller.

His clothes were almost dry now and he lost no time in putting them on. Holding the fish dangling from the line, he balanced himself between the two gunnysacks and urged the mule up and over the slope. When he rode into Grandma's yard, sweat was pouring from his face and the mule was in a lather. Grandma walked out to her porch, attracted by the noise.

"Shame on ye, Homer, runnin' that mule! What's wrong, is yore ma sick?"

"No," he answered, "Ma's sort of pindlin', but about the same as ever. You know what time it is, Grandma?"

"Sun is droppin' behind th' Chimneys. Goin' to be dark before ye know it. Ye ain't runnin' off are ye?" Grandma looked up, smiling.

Homer slipped to the ground and stood looking up at the ridge. "Runnin' off," he whispered. Grandma stepped from the porch and reached up to feel the sacks. Then she saw the fish.

"Lawsy me, Homer. Where in th' world did ye get such a fish? I ain't never seen one as big on th' mountain. Ye didn't ketch it yerself, did ye?"

Homer stood on one leg, fumbling the rope rein. The fish wasn't important now. He had promised his mother he would be home by noon and he had wasted the whole day away, leaving Ma to explain to Jed. Likely, Jed would give her the punishment meant for him. Grandma had asked if he was running away. The thought fitted into his mind as the best and only solution. He had been aiming to run off sooner or later, and now was as good a time as any.

"Yes, Granny," he answered, "I caught th' fish in th' river and I brung it to you. I guess I'll be travelin' toward Knob Ridge. Where ye want me to put these sacks of 'taters?"

"I see," Grandma said. "Well, you might as well put that mule in th' barn, set the 'taters in the corncrib, and then eat yourself some supper, Homer. You look mighty clean, honey. Want to milk my cow and bring some water from th' spring?"

When Homer finished the night chores, Grandma called him in to supper. He stood by the table covered with a red oilcloth, a pot of posies in the center, and stared at the savory dishes.

"Why, Granny, this place looks like the store of plenty th' Bible talks about. That table is too pretty to eat off!" Homer looked about him and saw the shelves filled with food.

"Set down and and help yourself. You ever see so nice a fish? It just about covers the platter. Take some of that hominy and them tomaters. Tomaters goes good with fish. I got a bread puddin' to finish off, puddin' with cream poured over." Grandma was proud. Homer was her first guest since her ship of plenty came in.

"You ain't drinkin' milk with that fish, Granny? Why it's poison," Homer exclaimed.

Grandma laughed. "Ain't nothin' to that talk, Homer. The fish is fresh and so is th' milk. Folks gets all kinds of crazy notions over eatin'. I eat anything I feel like eatin' and when I can get hold of it. I wish I could keep you here awhile and fatten ye up. You ain't as big as a sixteen-year-old boy ought to be."

"I'd like right well to be your boy, Granny. I don't want to move to th' valley. I might like to go down for a spell to see what it's like but I wouldn't want to stay. I don't hanker for all that level ground with no big trees, no huntin' or fishin'. If Pa was different, I'd get me a wife soon and homestead up here."

Homer reached for a saucer of puddin' and held it while Grandma poured over the cream. She tried hard not to smile.

"You talkin' of marryin'? Why I never heard of such a thing. You ain't long out of didies, Homer Simmons!"

Homer pushed back from the table, a flush mounting to his hair.

"I ought to know better than to talk man's talk to a woman. They never understand nothin'."

Now Grandma really did laugh. "When a man marries, Homer, it's to a woman," she said.

"Yeah, but a man don't marry a woman just to talk to her." Having decided definitely now to leave home for good, Homer found himself suddenly a man of independence, capable of opinions.

"According to your way of thinkin, a man marries a woman just to sleep with her," Grandma continued. Looking at him now, she saw his embarrassment. "Why, Homer, there ain't no call fer a man to be ashamed of nature. It gets a-hold of ye so, you ain't got no mind for nothing else and ye start after something blind as a bat. It's a urge that drives ye on and the thing I never will understand is why God didn't allow a little sense to walk along with that kind of nature. You don't know what it's all about till harm is done."

Grandma stood up to gather the dishes and Homer sat there and watched. There were a lot of things he'd like to know but he never thought he would ask a woman. Still, Grandma wasn't like any other woman. As far back as he could remember, she had lived alone and worked her place like a man.

"Grandma," he asked, "does a woman have nature just like a man?"

"Well," she answered, washing away at the dishes and keeping her back to Homer. "Ain't ye ever noticed the female beast, Homer? What about cows and dogs? Don't they have nature? I reckon a woman ain't no different from a cow. It's just that a cow or a beast has regular times and a woman don't. Is that what you're wantin' to know?'

It was what Homer wanted to know but he didn't answer right then. He had other questions.

"Granny," he asked, "if folks didn't have so many kids, it wouldn't be so hard to get along. Do they just have to have 'em? Ain't there no way?"

"If there is, I ain't heard of it, Homer. It's God's way. Some folks has more and some less. Ain't but one way to keep from havin' 'em and that's fer a man to let a woman alone, and I ain't ever seen a man that would."

Grandma opened the back door, threw the dishwater into the air, then hung the pan against the wall. She picked up the lamp and followed Homer into the cabin. Seating herself before the fire, she took out her pipe. "Homer," she said, "it's right fer a man to marry. It's God's way of meeting nature. But a man ought not to marry until he's strong enough to make a good livin' fer a woman and old enough to appreciate her. A woman ain't near strong enough to do all the work man piles on her. Pity is, a woman loves her man and so she takes the hardships of birthin', then out of the bed and right back to the same thing again."

"You see much of Jurie Biggers, Grandma?" he asked.

"Oh, so it's Jurie, is it?"

"None of that now, Granny. I don't reckon Jurie even knows I think about her. I ain't seen her since school last March. Jurie hates her pa, too, Grandma. He makes her do th' hardest work on that farm and they got a houseful of kids just like us. Looks like she's tied down to her ma and them young 'uns like I been. It ain't right."

"I don't reckon it would help matters if you give Juries another houseful of kids to 'tend to, Homer."

Homer laughed. "We might not have any kids a-tall, just like Tom and Callie."

Grandma grunted. "I wouldn't depend on that if I was you. Trifling with a girl ain't no way to do, Homer."

Homer leaped to his feet. "Good Gawd, Grandma! Yore mind is plumb evil, seein' nature in everything!"

Grandma smiled. "Well, it don't take much thinkin' to see it's all over you now, Homer. When a feller gets his mind goin' on such, and his body urgin' him on day after day, it's best fer him to make a change."

Grandma rose and knocked her pipe against the chimney. "Time fer bed, honey. I'll make ye a pallet here by the fire."

11

NEXT MORNING, Homer was just stepping from the barn
with the milk when he heard a mule on the road. Slipping
back, he placed the bucket on a shelf and climbed to the
loft. Peeping through the cracks he saw Jed ride into
Grandma's yard. A fear went over him and he was ashamed
of this fear, knew it wasn't right. He also knew if he had
any size in body he would face his father with confidence,
stand up for himself. Anger swelled in him, giving him a
feeling of recklessness. He had a good mind to go out there
and face Jed like a man, tell him that he had no intention
of going to the valley, and never again would he stand up
under the whip. Homer boiled, remembering the thrash-
ings, his father's drunken temper. Then he thought of his
mother and the little kids, always in fear of Jed. Homer
watched Grandma walk to the porch, wiping flour from
her hands. He pressed against the planks and listened.

"Grandma," Jed yelled, "seen anything of that trifling Homer?"

"What's wrong, Jed?" Grandma was evasive. "Is Marthy worse?"

"Naw, Marthy's all right but I'm plumb outdone with Homer. He run off with that mule and kept it out all night. I'm movin' today; got a truck to take our stuff down, but Homer has to drive the stock. Just wait till I get my hands on that kid!" Jed rode his mule up to the porch and looked at Grandma suspiciously, remembering her fondness for Homer.

"Well, don't stand there like a ninny! He's been around here, ain't he?" he yelled.

Grandma's eyes squinted to slits and her hands under her apron clenched into fists. From her window she had watched Jed ride up the hollow and while she knew he would be inquiring about Homer, still, Grandma had not anticipated this disrespect of her and right on the eve of Jed's movin'. Grandma had delivered all of Jed's children, even nursed him through a long illness in years past. There had been sickness among his children, injuries she had attended. And all that meant nothing to Jed. He didn't even have thanks inside him. Poor Marthy! No wonder Homer ran off. No wonder the boy was all mixed up inside himself, little and pindlin', slow in growing. God had sent that boy to her, and God would forgive her whatever means she must employ to protect him.

"I ain't seen a hair of Homer since I was at your house, Jed. Not a soul has passed this road in two days. I'm even surprised to see you, thought th' whole mountain had moved off. So fer as I'm concerned, the quicker you leave the better. You low-down rag of a man, not a drop of blood from your pa runs inside ye, Jed Simmons! Get outta my yard! Git, I say!" Grandma lifted her apron and shook it like a person shooing chickens.

Jed just sat there and laughed. "I reckon when winter closes ye in and nobody around fer ye to boss, you'll be callin' out with a different tune, Grandma." He turned the mule and called back, "What was that you said?"

"I said, pore Marthy, that's what I said. And I reckon a few months in that valley will cure you, too, Jed. Mark my words, you'll land in jail!" Grandma walked into her house, careful not to look toward the barn. Watching from the window, she saw Jed disappear over the far ridge, then she went to the door and called. "Come on to breakfast, Homer."

"That was a close shave, Grandma," he said, lifting the milk to the shelf. "I ain't goin' back home a-tall, now. It ain't that I'm scared to go; I'm just afraid I'll pick up something and kill Pa. I hate him, Granny!"

"Well, I can't blame ye much, Homer. But, try not to think about Jed, any more."

"This is th' best eatin' I ever had, Grandma. Them biscuits is as light as a feather. Ma never does feel like cookin' much and Effie ain't no good at a stove."

Grandma sat looking at Homer, loving him and wishing she could keep him with her. It would be a lonely winter for a boy with an old woman like her. Still, he had to go somewhere. Winter was just around the corner and he didn't even have a pair of shoes or a coat.

"Well, now your folks is movin' out, what ye plan to do, Homer?" she asked.

Homer walked to the door and stood looking out. Over that ridge was a short cut to the Biggers' place. A mile it was, and a mile wasn't anything.

"You aimin' to stay on th' mountain, Grandma?" he asked.

"Yep Ain't ye noticed my shelves full of winter grub? I traded my furniture for that. What ye gettin' at, Homer? You want to stay with me, is that it?" When Homer didn't answer right off, she thought maybe he couldn't bring himself to sponge off her.

"You'll have to work hard if you stay, Homer. There's wood to cut and a lot else. You can't always be runnin' over to th' Biggers."

"Aw, Grandma! Aaron said he was movin' to th' valley and that's what's worryin' me."

"I reckon I'll have to put your mind at ease, Homer. Tom Jenkins said Aaron was scared over movin' and likely it would be spring before he decided one way or the other. I think it's just meanness in Aaron, myself. He's holdin' out fer more money than th' Government wants to pay."

"Why, Grandma, everybody said you was against the folks movin' out. I heard you was even going to fight th' Government."

"I would, if folks hadn't moved off this way. What's th' use me settin' up here on th' mountain a-fightin' by myself, Homer? Of course I'm against th' folks movin' off. If I had years ahead of me, I'd do different. If ever' man on th' mountain had held out against the Government, I don't care what Doc Mayberry says, I don't believe even th' Government could have made 'em move."

Grandma looked at Homer and considered telling him

about her vision, of the times she had awakened in the night to see that big clock on her wall, the hands standing at twelve. Whether it was months or weeks, she didn't know. What she did know was that death lay close to her.

"Homer," she said, "life up here has changed more than 'you know."

"Tell me about th' old days, Granny."

"Th' part of livin' on Knob Ridge in years back is what you'd like to know."

"I never was up on Knob Ridge," Homer said, "but I heard about a old man from up there, name of Stillwater."

"Why, I know him. What about him, Homer? Is he dead?"

Homer laughed. "He wasn't dead last time I heard. His boy from th' valley come up to Knob Ridge and took him to his home, but old man Stillwater run off and come back to th' mountain. The other day he was over at th' store."

Grandma leaned back in her chair. "Well, well. I shore wish he'd come by here on his way home. He can tell stories ye wouldn't believe, Homer."

"You mean lies, Granny?" Homer got up from the table and reached for his cap.

"No, they ain't lies. It's th' truth. Where you goin'?"

"Oh, thought I'd slip over in th' woods back of our house and watch th' folks move off, Grandma. They might leave some things we could use. Ain't no feed in your barn for that cow and mule, and I got to get some, somehow."

"You mean you're goin' to stay with me up here?"

Homer walked over and touched Granny's shoulder. "If ye want me, I will."

"Sure, I want ye, honey."

Through the window, she watched Homer trot the mule down the slope and disappear in the woods, then went about her housework with a lighter heart than she had felt in weeks. She wasn't alone now. It was good having young ones about. They leaned on you, made a person feel useful.

When her house was clean and in order, the dinner cooking on the stove, she walked to the oak dresser and lifted out a bolt of bright outing cloth. This cloth, along with warm shoes, a sweater, gloves, wool stockings, and a rain cape, she had found in the new dresser drawer the doctor had left for her. No doubt he thought she would sew up a dress for herself from the outing. She would make two shirts for Homer. It came to Grandma all at once that her shoulder pain wasn't nearly so bad. She was sleeping better, too, but maybe that was because she now had something to eat. Suddenly, Grandma found herself singing. No particular song, just singing. A loud knock on her door stopped the shears in mid-air and she stood still, listening.

"Who is that?" she called.

"Open up, Grandma! We want to talk to ye."

That was Aaron Biggers' voice. Now what could he want of her? When she lifted the bar, Aaron pushed the door in and walked past her, followed by a man Grandma had never seen.

"Grandma," Aaron said, "I want to make ye acquainted with Lige Holder from up on Pine Ridge. He's got a message to pass around to hold us mountain folks together. Pull up a chair and set, Lige." Aaron took the one remaining chair himself, taking full command of the house. Grandma stood by the door and watched Lige tip back in his chair and look over her room, saw him draw a sack of

134

tobacco from his pocket.

"Nice place here, Biggers," he said.

Aaron looked around a bit startled over the change in Grandma's house. He wondered where she had got all this new stuff. "Yep," he answered, "we live right good in this cove." Then Aaron remembered Grandma.

"What's wrong with you, Grandma? Didn't ye hear me make ye acquainted with Lige Holder here? He's a big man on Pine Ridge." Aaron was ashamed of his neighbor before Lige. She was acting plumb mean and ornery. He ought to a-knowed better than to bring Lige over here. Grandma didn't have any sense any more, old and addle-brained.

So this is the man out to fight the Government, Grandma thought. Who was he, anyhow, to come into Weller Cove and tell folks what to do?

"Get me a chair, Aaron!" she ordered. Aaron sat there and stared, hostility in his eyes. Who ever heard of a woman bossing around like Grandma, and before Lige, too? Lige solved the matter by rising and giving Grandma his chair. She thanked him, and seated herself and reached for her pipe.

"Miz Weller," Lige began, "I hear you ain't set on movin' to the valley and I come over to lend my sympathy and advice and to show ye how ye can hold to your rights and keep your land. I'm sorry more of the folks don't see it this way, for then we could stand up against this robbery and bring a wholesale suit that would wreck the blasted state. There ain't no justice in it, Miz Weller. They ain't got a right in the world to take a man's land away from him. As long as there's a law in this country, we'll use it."

Lige was walking back and forth now before the hearth, delivering a lecture which months of practice had welded into an oration.

"No, sir-ree!" he shouted, pounding a fist in the palm of his hand, "the State of Tennessee will hear from me before I sell land that's been in my family for over a hundred years!" Stopping in front of Grandma, Lige pointed a finger and stated his next remark with fluttering whiskers and trembling voice. "I appealed to th' court over condemning my land by the powers of eminent domain, and you know what happened?" Lige's voice was now a bull's roar and Grandma flinched. "That case is goin' to the Supreme Court, that's what! I aim to get my rights and I aim to see that the rest of you folks gets yours, too. Somebody has to put a stop to this high-handed way of doing. It takes a leader, and that leader's me. I'm right behind ye, Miz Weller. What do ye think?"

Grandma took her pipe from her mouth. "I think," she said, "if you're behind me, I've gone cross-eyed. And I think if ye don't step from in front of that fire, I'm bound to spit on ye, certain." Grandma threw back her head and laughed uproariously. She had expected this visit from Lige Holder, but she had no idea he would be so ridiculous. Why, Lige didn't have the sense of a nanny goat!

Aaron leaped to his feet and stepped belligerently toward Grandma, but Lige stopped him with an arm. Motioning Aaron back to his seat, Lige leaned on the mantel, facing Grandma.

"You mean to tell me you're going to lay down and let the Government walk all over ye, let 'em take yore pa's house and move you out of the mountains, bag and

136

caboodle? I can understand such in the younger folks but not in us older ones who has been here since every ridge was thick with woods; since makin' a livin' was work such as them valley folks never heard tell of."

"I heard you been tryin' to sell your land fer ten years, Lige Holder. Looks to me like your feelings about th' mountain ain't set up right. You *did* try to sell it, didn't ye?" Grandma leaned over for the answer.

"Well," Lige hedged, "that ain't th' question, Miz Weller. There's a difference when somebody tries to take something away from ye."

"You mean you want to live on th' mountain, same as before? You mean it's because you're remembering your folks before you?"

"Who wants to live up here after everybody moves out?" Lige asked impatiently.

Grandma took a puff on her pipe and said, "I do. I aim to stay with my place and I don't care if th' whole tribe moves off and leaves me."

"And you aim to just take what them Government fellers offers fer your place, and whether it's a fair price or not."

Grandma remembered what Tom Jenkins had said, that the Government had offered Lige almost twice the amount he had been trying to get for his land.

"How much they offer for your place, anyhow?" she asked.

"Ten thousand dollars. That land of mine is worth fifteen thousand and I'll not sell it fer a cent less. What did they offer you, Miz Weller? I hear you got more land than anybody in this cove."

"They ain't been up here yet. And so fer as I see, you're

wastin' your time with me, Lige."

Lige struck a match to his cold pipe, considering another angle. Grandma had so much land the price would be a big one. As many cases in court as possible made the going better for him as well as the others he had aroused to fight. He guessed now that Grandma was so old she didn't have much sense.

"Miz Weller, you remember the neighborliness of the old days, lendin' and givin' and helpin' out when need come along? That's the core of this whole business now, being neighbors."

Grandma stopped her rocking. "Did you by any chance give this speech to Aaron before he jined up?"

Lige looked over at Aaron, who sat with folded arms and with a scowl that would have sharpened an axe. "Why, Aaron is as loyal a member as we've got, Miz Weller. He don't aim to give over his place unless it appears justice is done. He ain't set on takin' his family to th' valley to starve on no pittance. Why, he can keep 'em alive and healthy up here, and where his pa set an example before him."

Grandma laughed. "I reckon I know Aaron better than you do, Lige. I knowed his pa and his great-pa, too. They is all alike, the Biggers clan. They always aimed to get their money's worth and no matter what. Aaron ain't burnin' with feelings for his folks who died before him. Aaron is thinkin' just of Aaron."

Aaron barged to his feet and walked to the door. "I'll wait with th' team, Lige. Why don't you leave that old fool alone! She's crazy as a bedbug and everybody in this cove knows it."

Grandma reached to the hearth for a coal. "Listen here,

Lige," she said, stopping long enough to light her pipe. "I been hearin' a lot of things about you and I was hopin' you'd come around so I could know how you feel. I don't mind tellin' ye that I'm downright disappointed in ye. I had the idee you was loyal to your land and wanted to stay with it, that you was tryin' to get other folks to stay, too. If that was so, then there would be a principle in what you're doin'. As it is, you're holding things upside down and wrongside out."

When Lige didn't answer, Grandma went on. "I ain't crazy, like Aaron said. I been thinkin' a lot about this business and when them Government fellers gets to me, I'll make the price myself. I don't never make up my mind out of other folks's idees. Another thing, Lige, you are a stranger to me and to this cove. I been here nearly a hundred years and I never set eyes on you before. How come you get so all-fired much interest in what happens to me and my place? How come you bring that Aaron Biggers over, pretendin' to help me? When I see Aaron settin' out to do anything for another person, I know something is wrong."

Grandma rose from her rocker. "Nope!" she declared, "you just go on bein' a leader on Pine Ridge all ye want to, Lige. Aside from Aaron, I don't reckon you'll find a single person in this cove who'll listen to your preachin' ways! I ain't followin' nobody. I'm by way of bein' a leader, too, if ye don't know it. Bein' a woman, I reckon that goes against your grain, eh, Lige?"

Grandma closed her mouth on her pipe and walked toward her kitchen. She had no more to say. She allowed Lige expected an invite to dinner. Well, he could expect on. She wasn't goin' to counsel none of that business, settin' to the table with traitors.

Lige stepped to the door and called back, "You're all mixed up and contrary, Grandma Weller. I reckon you don't know Bud Latham's on our side, too. Just wait till them Government fellers gets to you and you'll change yore tune. They ain't goin' to put up with yore sassy ways. They won't give ye time to make up yore mind because they'll make it up for ye!"

The door closed with a bang and Grandma stood by her stove, hearing the mules trot down the road.

Bud Latham, the silly old fool, she thought. Likely as not, Polly had already gone to the valley and them fellers had Bud steamed up with liquor. Well, it was a good thing she had not depended on Bud.

Grandma walked to the back door and looked out. The sky was overcast with fast-moving clouds. She glanced up at the Chimney Tops and saw the faint outline of the peaks waver and then disappear behind a veil of smoky mist. She watched the clouds lower, spread through the cove. It was always different, she thought. For ninety years she had watched those mountains and never two days did they appear the same. Grandma could tell weather signs from the mountaintops. She held her hand out now and felt a fine drizzle of rain. She wondered why she dreaded winter so much this year? She never had before.

Grandma heard a strange noise and, looking down, she found the answer to a problem that had worried her for three weeks.

"Why, Daisy, you old fool hen! Ain't ye got a bit o' sense? Hidin' off and hatchin' a family at the very start of winter!" Grandma counted fifteen fluffy chickens as they ran. She stepped down and Daisy gathered her brood at Grandma's feet.

"Get in that house, Daisy, and stop that fussin'! Ye knowed right well ye could depend on me. That's why ye done it." Stooping, Grandma gathered the chicks in her apron. "Come on!" she ordered, and Daisy hopped up the steps and followed her into the kitchen as she had done times before. Grandma placed the chicks in a box behind the stove, then crumbled corn bread for them.

"Oh, so ye don't trust me, eh?" Daisy had hopped to the box to peep over the side. Grandma fondled her pet hen, laughing. Then she turned to dinner. This old stove was just worn out, Grandma decided. It was so open and drafty it ate wood like a hungry wolf. It was cantankerous and poured heat in the oven when and if it felt like it. All things got worn out with time, Grandma thought.

She looked around her kitchen now with pride. It came to her that if Homer was to live with her all winter, she had better ration the grub and try to be thrifty. Homer would make his board in more ways than one. She would make a man out of him this winter, that is, if Jed didn't find out about him and come and take him away.

12

A LOUD *whoa!* from the back yard made Grandma know Homer was back. So Jed didn't get his hands on the boy after all. She smiled and opened the door. What Grandma saw was a shock. There was Homer sitting on top a wagon-load of corn and hay, and numerous other boxes and bundles tied on at the back.

"Homer!" Grandma gasped. "Ain't that yore pa's wagon?"

Homer laughed, seeing Grandma's face so surprised and pleased.

"It was Pa's wagon once, but I reckon it's ours now, unless he takes it away from us. Judging from weather signs today," he said, looking up at the sky, "I reckon gettin' a wagon and team down that slick mountain road is something Pa will put off fer a while. If winter would come in suddenlike, Grandma, we'd be pretty safe till spring."

Grandma looked over toward the mountains. "Well, I wouldn't be a bit surprised if winter don't ride in any day now." Lifting her apron around her head, she limped to the wagon. Homer jumped down and began to lift off his prize packages.

"Here's a pretty good hoe and a bucket of nails. Here's a screen off a winder and a good winder sash. I brought a bed ticking Ma left on th' line. Thought I could fill it with straw and make me a bed. Found a pair of Pa's old shoes. I can make 'em do me fer a while. I brought th' old washtub. It leaks, but I can melt some lead and fix it. Here's a sack of cement, Granny; I aim to see if I can mend your stove so it holds heat better. Here's some turnip seed and I picked all the green tomaters. There's a bushel of 'em. Thought you might want to make pickles. Some ripe ones in there fer seed. Got some odds and ends like cans and buckets, an old saw and a grindstone. I'll have to sharpen your axe before I can cut wood."

All the time Homer was lifting the things to the ground, Grandma stood there, her heart churning. It had been so many years since Ethan was here doing things for her, she had almost forgotten what it was like to have companionship. It seemed she never had time to go about making her house comfortable for all needs. Most any time and in the middle of a task, she was likely to be stopped and called to a neighbor's house miles away, sickness or a new baby being born. Homer laid the last of his bundles on the ground, and started to drive on to the barn and unload the corn and hay. All at once, he realized that Grandma had said not a word, and he turned. When he saw tears on her face, he stood startled for a moment, then stepped to her side.

"Why, Granny, I ain't hurt ye, have I?" he asked.

Grandma put her arms around him and drew him to her. "No, honey, I'm just thinkin' how nice it is to have a boy thinkin' of my comforts and doin' fer me. Seems nobody has cared in an awful long time. I hadn't thought much about it before now. but I reckon I been lonesome, Homer."

"No need to be lonesome now, Grandma. I'm here with ye and I'm goin' to stay as long as ye want me." Homer smiled. "I laid out in th' woods and watched 'em move off, Granny. Then I slipped over and got these things. Got my rifle, too. I hid it under the house. There's an old hen settin' under there on a dozen eggs. I left corn scattered fer her."

"Well, you'd better unload that stuff and come get some hot dinner, Homer. You must be powerful hungry and you're cold and wet, too." Grandma picked up the bed ticking and walked up the steps.

Turning the mule into a stall, Homer threw in corn for him and for old Bess, then he walked across the barn lot toward the cabin. He stood by the woodpile, worried. Hardly enough to keep the kitchen stove going a week. He had little time to gather all the wood needed for two fires and for a whole winter. It was going to be a rush job. If he just had somebody to help him with a crosscut saw. With just an axe, it was going to be slow work and he'd better get started.

Homer stepped into the kitchen and laughed loud over Daisy. "What ye know about that?" he exclaimed. Daisy was clucking disapproval. "She don't like me, Grandma."

"Oh, I reckon she'll get used to ye, Homer. Come on and drink some of this bean soup while it's hot. Crumble some of that corn pone in it. That boiled bacon goes good, too. I got a apple pie fer ye, Homer." Homer looked up and smiled.

"Wish ye was a young girl, Granny, I'd marry ye in a minute."

Grandma laughed. "I reckon if I was a young girl, I wouldn't mind a bit, Homer."

The little kitchen was warm and full of savory odors. It filled Homer with a peace and contentment he had never before experienced. He thought about his mother and the little children going down to live in a strange country among strange folks. Grandma watched, knowing full well his thinking.

"Worryin' over yore ma, honey?" she asked.

"I reckon I am, Granny. I guess maybe I wouldn't a-run off, except Pa bought a place in the valley with just twenty-five acres. Not much winter work on a place that little, and Joe's fourteen now."

"You expectin' yore pa to come back up here, huntin' ye up?" she asked.

"Wouldn't be surprised a bit. Only thing, he'll be too busy gettin' settled at first. I'm hopin' by th' time he gets to it, winter will be along. That makes me think of wood, Grandma. I got to get to that wood right away. Wish I had somebody to help me with a crosscut saw."

"Reckon ye might get Tom Jenkins fer a day or so?" she suggested.

"I saw Tom on th' road, and he needs help hisself."

"When's him and Callie leavin'?"

"He said they didn't aim to go till next week, but with the weather like it is he thinks best to get off as soon as possible. He offered me a dollar to come over this evenin' and help out. Sam Acree left yesterday. I aim to ride around and see what everybody left at all the places. I might find things we need, Grandma. Shucks, wish I could see Jurie and find out what Aaron plans to do."

"Homer," Grandma warned, "you'd better be careful till winter sets in. Aaron wouldn't like nothin' better than to send word to Jed about your bein' up here with me. Anyhow, I don't know as you should go to all this trouble around here. Supposin' them Government fellers comes around and tells me to move off? I reckon all this plannin' for winter comforts would be for nothin'. I wish I knew fer certain. Looks like I can't get settled in mind a-tall. I wish Lige Holder had stayed home where he belongs."

Homer looked up in surprise. "He been over here?"

"Yep. Him and Aaron come today. Seems th' Government wants to use some of the land and not everybody can stay on. Makes me so mad I don't know what to do."

"What if they said they wanted your place, Granny? What would ye do?"

"I'd say just to want on, that I ain't leavin' my home."

"Then, what ye want to worry for?" Homer asked.

"I'm a-feared I'll die before they come, Homer. That way, they might just take my place and not pay nothin' fer it. That ain't right."

"What did Aaron say?" Homer asked, afraid the Biggers would move off before he could see Jurie.

Grandma sniffed. "Nothin' Aaron Biggers says means anything to me. If I was a man, I'd think twice before hitchin' up to them Biggers. There's bad blood there,

Homer, and blood tells."

Homer rose from the table, laughing. "I reckon you ain't seen Jurie since she growed up, Grandma. She ain't like Aaron. Anyhow, I'll have to leave courtin' be till I get things fixed fer winter around here. Maybe there ain't no use in doing too much fixin', Grandma, but we got to have wood."

"Best put some gunnysacks around your shoulders, Homer. We've got to figure on gettin' you a coat of some kind."

He hurried with his work that night. Funny how different living was over at Grandma's. Back at home he never did anything right and, like as not, a licking would be waiting for him at the end of the day.

Homer stepped from the barn, his eyes turning to the ridge. If he just had the wood cut, then he would go about looking up Jurie. He wondered how a feller went about courting a girl. He was so occupied with his thoughts, he didn't hear a noise on the road. He looked up startled, no time to hide. Aaron Biggers pulled his mule to a stop in the road and sat there, staring. Homer raised his hand in salute and Aaron moved on down the road toward home. "Son of a bitch!" Homer swore under his breath. Pore Jurie, he thought.

Looking toward the cabin, Homer was startled to see a strange mule tied to a porch post. He ran back to the barn, peeped through a crack in the planks, studying the mule. It wasn't Jed's mule, unless he had bought another one and Homer was sure he hadn't. Whoever had ridden that mule was in Grandma's house right now. No doubt he had come along with Aaron.

"Homer!"

Grandma was calling him. That meant it was safe, no danger in showing himself. He gathered an armload of wood from the yard and opened the kitchen door to a flood of laughter.

"This is Grampy Stillwater, Homer. I sure am glad to see him."

Homer dropped the wood in the box, and walked over to shake hands with the oldest man he had ever seen. Grampy's face was covered with white whiskers, his body long and thin. He was wearing a pair of new overalls, an old sweater. His brown eyes were soft and gentle like Grandma's.

"Howdy, Grampy," Homer said. "Don't you tell any stories until I get back from milking."

Grandma laughed. "I reckon Still couldn't tell all the tales he knows if he talked all winter. He's been tellin' me about the valley. We're waitin' supper on you, Homer."

Homer reached for the milk bucket and ran to the barn and into the cow stall.

"Saw-Bess. Move over, ye old heifer. I'm in a hurry." Bess looked around, chewing noisily, and switched her tail through the air to wrap itself around Homer's neck.

Dad blast it! Nothing moved right and easy when time was short. Homer set the bucket on the ground, squatted, and buried his head in the cow's flanks. Damned if he didn't forget to wash his hands like Grandma said. He spread his fingers before grabbing hold the teats. No feller as skinny as him could have such big hands. He wished to Gawd he'd start growing. Those big hands took hold the teats now and milk streamed into the bucket. Homer guessed he had milked cows a million times.

148

13

"As I was sayin'," Grampy said, leaning back in his chair, "I told this here story to them missionary women at Sary's."

"What is missionary women?" Grandma wanted to know.

"Why, it's a lot o' womenfolks gettin' together to sew and make clothes fer pore folks around. It's 'cause they ain't got nothing else to do. Reminds me of Mattie Green-law back on Knob Ridge. Mattie went to th' valley to visit her girl and come back with all sorts o' crazy notions. She got all the women organized in a sassiety fer lookin' after th' pore." Grampy snickered. "Trouble was, there warn't no pore folks around right then. But they kept on a-meetin' and a-cannin' and waitin' fer a pore family to come along. Well, after a time a strange family come in on foot and took up in the mill cabin on Mossy Creek. Mattie went over there one day and come back all excited and said, 'Glory be, we got some pore folks at last!'"

"Where'd them folks come from?" Homer asked.

"Well, Homer, nobody knowed. Back on Knob Ridge people don't ask questions of strangers. This feller's name was Jimpson and he was mean as a snake. Ye could tell that by just lookin' at him and he never went anywhere without his gun. He wouldn't take up with nobody and we left him alone. It was th' womenfolks that started it, feelin' sorry fer that Jimpson woman and a house full of naked young 'uns."

"What happened?" Grandma asked, interested.

"Why this is all about Heeb Tanner, Grandma. You remember about his leg?" Grandma nodded.

"Now, them womenfolks allowed it might be a good idea to get Heeb Tanner to go with 'em to that pore family, what with Heeb bein' a sort of preacher on Knob Ridge. They conjectured a little prayin' might set well and put th' hand of the Lord in the dish of givin' and make them pore folks aware of their blessings. Five women started out with Heeb, but passin' ever' house, somebody else jined th' bunch, curious mostly. By th' time they reached the mill, there was twenty of 'em in all. When they turned into the gate, Heeb raised his voice to sing and all th' rest strung along with him. They was singin' 'Count Yore Blessings.'"

Grandma laughed. "I reckon that started somethin'. Heeb should a-had more sense."

"It shore did start somethin'," Grampy said. "That feller Jimpson was standing on his porch holding a shotgun. He looked so mean and so cussed mad, them women sort of hung back and somebody told Heeb to pray. Heeb stepped up to th' porch all filled with th' spirit and raised his voice.

" 'Like manna that fell from the skies in th' desert, like fish that come from a loaf of bread, like water that run from th' rock o' Moses.' Heeb sure knew his Bible but he didn't get no further than that. That feller Jimpson yelled out, 'What in hell is goin' on around here?'

"That sorter stumped pore old Heeb. 'Why, we heard luck was down on ye, brother, and thought to share our goods and give ye a start.' That's what Heeb said.

"That feller Jimpson raised that gun, pinted it at Heeb, and pulled th' trigger."

"Gawd Almighty!" Homer exclaimed. "The dirty skunk!"

"Oh, it didn't kill him. That gun was filled with buckshot and the blast hit Heeb just over th' knee. Them women forgot all about bein' afraid, then. They picked Heeb up, and took him in th' mill cabin, and went about doctorin' him. Word went around and the men began to gather. That scared Jimpson. He knew if Heeb died, the fellers would string him up. So one night he slipped out back and got away. I don't know yet how he done it, what with a wife and them kids. It may be some of th' fellers knew it and considered it a good loss. Anyhow, nobody followed him. Everybody was worried over Heeb."

"Heeb died, didn't he?" Homer asked.

"No, he didn't die but he lost his leg. They spent five days tryin' to find a feller willin' to cut off that leg, but nobody'd do it. And all th' time old Heeb was dyin' of poison. He knew it, too. He begged and he prayed and it didn't do no good. Finally he give up and started callin' fer a knife and a saw. He called fer a pair of pinchers and some red-hot pokers. He called fer rags, hot water, and a quart of whiskey."

"Is that so, you reckon, Granny?" Homer asked.

"Course it's so, Homer. Ain't you got no manners?"

Homer looked at Grampy. "I didn't mean no harm," he said.

"No harm's done, Homer, I ain't surprised. Ye see, them valley women wouldn't believe this story, neither. It was right at this point that Sary got up and went to her kitchen fer refreshments fer them missionary women. And she told me to shut up or nobody would want any of her grub." Grampy laughed, remembering.

"Now, back to Heeb Tanner," he went on. "They sent word fer miles around and set th' day of th' cuttin' on a Saturday. Folks rode muleback for thirty miles and brought grub to last a week. Dave Pratt brought enough whiskey to float a house. And, Grandma, you sent a jug o' herb medicine and said to soak that stump in it and keep it soaked."

Grandma nodded, remembering.

"I wrapped up that stump myself," Grampy said. "If I had it to do over again, I'd a-cut off Heeb's leg. I can still see pore old Heeb. He started in to prayin' and to drinkin'. It was the first time he ever took whiskey in his life. I never will understand it, but it took near a whole quart to get him good and drunk. When he got drunk, he started in to singin' and he wanted to throw a square dance right there. We had to tie him to th' plank."

"What plank?" Homer asked.

"Why, we took th' barn door down and set it up on trestles in the middle of th' cabin. Heeb said he wanted noise, so th' fellers got out their harps and fiddles and ye never heard such music in all yore born days. Eph Trooby from Pine Ridge just outfiddled hisself that night. I reckon Eph was more help to Heeb than anybody else.

"We had four pokers red hot in the fire, all set to sear and stop th' blood. We had a wad of cobwebs and some mud made up with spit. We had rags, hot water, and needles and thread. We even had a crosscut saw. We got the biggest butcher knife on the mountain and honed it to a quick edge and then we het it red hot in th' fire. Everything was all set and ready, folks' nerves as sharp as that butcher knife.

"All at once one of th' fellers yelled, 'Go to it, Heeb! Git it over with for Gawd's sake!'

"Poor old Heeb was settin' there on that plank, grinnin' and lookin' foolish. His face was red as fire, fer he had a high fever as well as a quart o' liquor inside him.

" 'Hand me a piece of charcoal,' Heeb called out. 'I want to mark th' spot. Why, damn it, I might cut off the wrong leg!'

"Heeb picked up that butcher knife then, and all us fellers moved in close to see th' blood fly. He laid the knife down on that leg and you could a-heard a straw hit th' floor, it was so quiet. All at once, he throwed that knife across the cabin. It stuck pint-blank in a log and hung there, tremblin'.

" 'Oh, Gawd, I can't do it!" he yelled. 'Get the axe and cut it off in one full swoop!' He started cryin' then, and everybody in the whole house began to blubber. Only Eph

Trooby kept up th' fiddlin' and Eph was as white as a sheet."

Grampy stopped his story to lean and light his pipe.

"But that's not all th' story," Homer said. "Heeb did cut off his leg, didn't he?"

"Naw, he didn't. Eph Trooby throwed down that fiddle and before ye could say jackrabbit, that leg of Heeb's hit th' floor. I can't remember which hit th' floor first, that leg or Eph. He went out like a light."

Grampy laughed, seeing Homer's expression. He looked over at Grandma, puffing gently on her pipe.

"Wish I'd a-been there," she said. "I'd a-cut off his leg. I've cut two legs off in my time. Ye say ye told that story to them valley women?" she asked.

"Yes, but they didn't believe it, jest made 'em sick to th' stummick, is all. Made me sick, too, when Sary came in with that grub."

"What was it?" Homer asked.

"Meat with tomato ketsup poured over it."

Grandma leaned back and laughed. Grampy joined in.

"That's why I had to leave," Grampy said, rising to knock out his pipe on the hearth. "I'm kinder tired and wore out, Grandma. Ye got any covers fer a pallet?"

"Sure I have. Homer, fix your bed ticking fer Still."

Homer sat there looking at Grampy, disbelief in his eyes. "You swear to Gawd that's so, Grampy?" he asked.

"Gawd A'mighty! Even my own folks thinks me a liar!" Then Grampy laughed. "Sure, it's so, Homer. I can tell ye worse things than that. I'll tell ye one tomorrow afore I leave."

Homer lay on a pallet before the fire, hearing snores in

154

the cabin: Grandma in her brass bed and Grampy on the bed tick. Outside, he could hear the wind in the pine tree next the cellar. A cold draft moved along the floor and he shivered, thinking about the firewood.

14

NEXT MORNING Homer walked into the kitchen, setting the milk bucket on the table. "Gettin' cold as kraut outside," he said. "I got to sharpen that axe and get to cuttin' wood."

"And I got to saddle up that mule and get on home," Grampy said, pushing back from the table. "Best eatin' I had in a long time, Grandma. Looks like you're fixed right comfortable for winter. I'd like to buy a bottle of that rheumatiz tonic if ye got any to spare."

"Sure, I got plenty in th' cellar. But I wish you'd stay on with us, here. Seems like talkin' to ye is the most natural livin' I've had in a long time."

"You ain't goin' afore ye tell that story ye promised, Grampy?" Homer asked. "Come on, tell it now while I eat. Then I'll saddle th' mule and bring him around."

"Might as well get it over," Grandma said, reaching for

the cloth to strain the milk. "Homer plagues me for stories of th' old days. Another thing, Still, I ain't takin' no money fer that tonic."

Grampy laughed. "Oh, yes, ye are. This is the only time I ever had any money to pay debts with. Why, I'll die afore I get it all spent, anyhow. Besides, Grandma, you've been sending me tonics for going on sixty year and I never give you nothin'." Grampy opened his purse and laid a ten-dollar bill on the table.

Grandma stood there looking at the bill. "Well," she said, reaching for it, "if you're sure ye can spare it, then I can use it right well. Ye say you plan to live by yourself up on the Ridge, Still? Supposin' ye get sick or something?"

"Oh, there's other folks stayin' with th' land on Knob Ridge. Anyhow, I got to go back, Grandma. I got to be there when th' spring wind blows. I hope when I come to die, it'll be in the spring."

"What about th' spring?" Grandma asked, taking a chair.

"Well, that's a story, Grandma. I reckon it's th' story Homer wants to hear. I ain't never told it before and it'll take a little time and maybe ye ain't got time to hear it, Homer."

Homer mopped up the last of the sorghum with a biscuit and pushed back his chair. "I'll take time, Grampy, and I'd sure like to hear it."

Grampy looked out the window, a dreamy expression in his eyes. "There ain't no place on th' mountain like Knob Ridge. It's on account of th' wind. In th' winter it howls and it roars. It creeps under th' eaves and it whistles in th' chimney. Then, when a thaw comes, there's a steady drip-

drip of icicles from the pine trees. Th' spring wind is like a
great big fan. It comes even and steady like music. If you
listen real good, you can tap your foot, just like with a
fiddle. But most of all, th' spring wind is like a woman
singing to a baby and ye can hear th' cradle rockin'.''

"You mean that's how it sounds to you, eh, Grampy?"
Homer asked.

"I mean no such thing. It sounds that way to everybody
up there, and there's a reason. I'm goin' to tell ye why now
and don't ye interrupt me, either.

"Back on Knob Ridge there used to be a feller named
Ace Lemmon. Nobody knowed where Ace come from
'cause he didn't talk much. I reckon Ace done all his
talkin' on a fiddle, for never before nor since could any
feller pour out such tunes, just makin' 'em up as he sawed
along.

" 'Work up a windstorm, Ace,' the fellers would ask, and
Ace would smile and raise his bow. If you closed your eyes
to listen, you could hear that storm comin' across the valley. First it was far off, like a moan, low and full of bass,
then, little by little it began to whine. After a while it rose
to a roar, whipping through the hollers and in and out the
trees.

"Now Ace was a wiry little feller and as spry as a flea. He
could do more work in less time than any man on the
mountain. Lief Tatum said it was because Ace wanted to
get back to that fiddle. He lived by hisself and he never did
take a wife. When fellers asked him why, Ace laughed and
said a woman would keep him working in th' corn rows
and when it came to choice, he'd take his fiddle.

" 'Play a cat-and-dog fight, Ace," the kids would ask, and

Ace would pick up that fiddle and make hounds bark and yelp and cats meow and screech.

"But th' best things on Ace's fiddle was th' songs he played and sung. He must a-made 'em up hisself, fer nobody ever heard 'em before. All the singin' us folks did was songs we'd heard all our lives and everybody knew 'em. That's why Ace's songs set so well. Ever' time anything happened on th' mountain, Ace made it into song.

"The fellers thought he must a-loved a woman once, for he sung one song more than any other, but only when he thought he was by hisself.

"I could tell ye a lot o' stories about Ace but this has to do with the strangest happening ever come to Knob Ridge. Makes me ashamed and yet, it might be that pore old Ace had to be a lamb of th' slaughter.

"Now it come around to sorghum-makin' time and it was a growin' year fer cane. About ten of us fellers was gathered at old Lief Tatum's to help him out. Ace was there, settin' off to th' side with his fiddle, a-playin' and a-singin'. Sometimes a feller's axe would ring out, choppin' wood fer the fire. He'd swing that axe with th' tune, so it was like keepin' time with a drum. Lief would stir and skim and even his wooden spoon moved with the fiddle. We took the barn door down so Jake Trooby could strut a turkey wing. Jake was as limber as a string and as long-legged as a grasshopper. The way that boy's feet could fly was a sight on earth to watch.

"It was gettin' along close to night and the last batch of sorghum was ready. I remember the womenfolks had made candy sticks of th' sorghum and was passin' 'em 'round. I remember Ace walkin' over to th' water bucket and standin' there with th' gourd in his hand, listening.

"Ace had an uncommon good hearin', fer it was a minute or so before I heard anything above the sputterin' of the fire and th' boilin' of th' molasses. But it come to me then, a horse on th' road and traveling at breakneck speed. Everybody turned to look and it wasn't long until we made out Jud Haley on his roan stallion.

"Jud almost run over us, pullin' that horse to a stop. He leaped to the ground and that's the first time we noted he had a gun.

" 'Where's Ace Lemmon?' he shouted.

" 'Why I'm right here,' Ace said, stepping up surprised. Jud raised that gun and he'd a-killed Ace right there if Lief hadn't reached out and knocked up th' barrel. The gun exploded, then all the fellers was on Jud and bore him to th' ground.

" 'You crazy Jud Haley? What in hell is wrong with you, anyhow?' That was Lief Tatum.

"Jud lay there on th' ground lookin' up at us and, all at once, he started bawlin'. It's awful to hear a man cry.

" 'It's Winnie!' Jud sobbed. 'Ain't nothin' but a kid, just a baby, ruined, and by a man who goes around fiddlin'; and a-makin' folks think—'

"Ace Lemmon stepped up. 'Look here, Jud Haley, you accusin' me of trifling with a girl like Winnie? My Gawd!' Ace looked around to see if us fellers would stand up fer him, but nobody said a word. We all just stood there lookin' from Ace to Jud. I don't know what the other fellers thought but I was rememberin' how Winnie was always goin' down to Ace's cabin to sing and dance to the fiddle. She was a purty little trick, about fourteen and with hair the color of copper. Winnie's the only girl I ever seen with red eyes but they went good with her hair and her white skin. Maybe all the other fellers thought like I did, I don't know. Jud got up then and sat on a box and said, 'Winnie said it was you, Ace.'

"Ace just stood there, lookin' to me like a man drunk. He moved his eyes from one to another of us, hunting a friend, I reckon. There ain't much a man can do when a woman accuses him, 'specially if it's just a girl like Winnie. Ace said a strange thing then. 'I shore am sorry, Jud. If I was Winnie's pa, I'd feel the same way.'

"Jud jumped up and started for Ace with his fists, but Lief stood between them.

" 'Git outta my way, Lief Tatum! Ye heard him admittin' it, didn't ye?' he shouted.

" 'No,' Lief said, 'I didn't hear no such thing. A feller can make mistakes by goin' too fast, Jud.'

"Jud went back and sat down again, and everybody looked at Ace, waitin' fer him to deny it. Time passed and it seemed like Ace was thinking up a good story to disprove hisself, even as he stood there before th' fellers as guilty as hell. I know now that Ace was waitin' fer the fellers to speak fer him. He thought his livin' amon'st us was all that was needed if character has anything to do with habit. I was just a kid then, about fourteen, but I think I growed up that night. I stood there and watched hope slip off Ace Lemmon's shoulders and drop to the ground at his feet. His face was like a page in th' Bible and you could read it out loud. There was hurt written there, written so deep it burned in Ace's eyes like embers in hot ashes. I saw lines form at the edge of his hair and run down his cheeks, settin' his mouth all crooked and a-quiver.

" 'Say somethin', Ace,' Lief Tatum asked.

" 'There ain't but one thing to say, Lief.' Ace spoke so low we hardly made out his words. 'I'm sorry about Winnie, sorrier than you fellers'll ever know. But I reckon something else hurts me, too, and if you don't know what it is, then I ain't got no more to say.'

"Jud Haley stood to his feet. 'Come on, fellers, and let's string him up!' he yelled.

"Ace just stood there, and I saw him holdin' his fiddle close to him as if to get comfort somewhere.

" 'We ain't never hanged a man fer such a thing yet, Jud,' Lief Tatum said. 'There's a better way. Let Ace marry Winnie tonight.'

" 'No! I ain't goin' to marry Winnie, 'cause . . .' Ace stopped and it looked like he was going to deny Winnie's charge, but he never did deny it.

" 'Let's all set down right here and think this think out,' Lief Tatum said, more stirred than I ever knew him to be. Lief was a old feller, a sort of leader on Knob Ridge. Us folks looked to th' old ones, then, to tell us what to do.

" 'Killin' a feller is bad business and I don't hold with it,' Lief said. 'Let a man live his punishment. As fer Ace, th' only thing that means anything to him is that fiddle. Let's take his fiddle away from him.'

"Jud spoke up real quick then. 'Hell, what good would that do? He could get another fiddle, couldn't he? Let's cut off his bow hand!'

"A rumble moved over the crowd and I heard one of the womenfolks cry out, 'Oh, no! Oh, Gawd, no!'

"I stood there lookin' at Ace Lemmon and even the

162

Lord couldn't have showed more grief when Judas stood before him. Ace looked down at his fiddle, huggin' it close to his side. He even spread his hand and clenched his fingers to a fist like he was seein' if that right hand was still there.

" 'Well, what are we waitin' fer, anyhow? Let's get goin'!' Jud stood up and the crowd got to millin'. The womenfolks set to moanin' and cryin'. 'Don't let him do it, Lief! Don't let him do it!'

"Lief turned to the fellers then, and said, 'Th' kind of music Ace plays and the words he makes into songs ain't earthly. A Spirit, higher up, touches that bow hand.' Then Lief straightened to his full height and looked us over, anger in his lined face and a quiver in his voice.

" 'I call Gawd to witness my words, to put a restraining hand on you, Jud Haley. And all the rest of you who rush to this punishment and take it into your own hands, you'll live to rue th' day, so help me, Gawd!'

"Lief turned then and went in his house and closed his door. The molasses boiled on till it was set and hard and no use to anybody. One by one the fellers saddled up and rode away and nobody turned to look back. I was th' last left, save Jud and Ace and the womenfolks belonging at Lief's. The women was off to th' side cryin'. Jud set there with his eyes on Ace, brooding, I reckon on what Lief had said.

" 'Much rather you just shot me, Jud,' Ace said.

"Jud laughed in his throat and it was a mean sound. 'You would eh? Then shootin's too good fer ye. No, we'll make it that bow hand and make it quick.' Jud got up and reached for the axe. A woman screamed in the crowd, 'Let

163

him play a song, Jud. Let him play.' I reckon that woman thought a song, right then, might turn Jud's heart. Jud stood there with the axe in his hand and Ace lifted his fiddle. Th' song Ace sung was one he must a-made up on the minute, fer I never heard it before.

> There's a land across th' river,
> A land I'm going to see,
> So I pick me up my fiddle
> 'Cause my fiddle goes with me.
> And I'll step upon th' water
> Like th' Man of Galilee,
> And I'll fiddle, fiddle, fiddle all th' way.

> When I reach the land of Jordan
> I'll fiddle all day long
> And I'll fiddle on th' mountain
> In a woman's cradle song.
> When the spring wind comes a-ridin'
> You'll know ye done wrong
> For I'll fiddle, fiddle, fiddle all the way.

"When Ace started his song I could see it had effect on Jud but when he reached the part about a cradle and a woman singing to a baby, that brought th' whole thing back. Jud held the axe in one hand and shot out his fist with the other. Ace rose in the air, being a little feller. His fiddle sailed out and I caught it before it hit the ground. And strange as may be, when Ace struck earth his right hand fell across a log just like a chicken's neck on a choppin' block. Jud raised that axe and severed Ace's bow hand as clean as a whistle.

"I remember looking at big Jud Haley and being

ashamed for not doing something to stop him. I felt cowardly and disloyal to Ace, whom I loved although I wasn't nothing but a boy. I stood there and didn't know I was cryin' till I tasted salt on my tongue. I didn't even hear a wagon on th' road. I saw the womenfolks run over to aid pore old Ace and then I saw Winnie jump from the wagon and rush over to him.

" 'Oh, Gawd!' she said. 'What have I done? Oh, Pa! Oh, Ace!'

"Winnie fainted then and Jud caught her in his arms. I never in all my life seen such a look on a man's face, for Jud knew then that Ace was not th' one and maybe he was rememberin' Lief Tatum's words. His face turned gray and his whole body sagged like a meal sack. Winnie just slid out o' his arms, and lay on the ground beside Ace. Jud looked around at us all.

" 'Gawd forgive me,' he said. Then he turned, unhitched his stallion and was off down the road in a cloud o' dust.

"Well this story goes on and covers twelve months and, fer that matter, that story still goes on and it's been nearly eighty years since it happened. Lief Tatum's womenfolks had to keep and care for Winnie, for Jud wouldn't let her come home after that, nor would he let her name be spoke in his presence. And as fer Ace, he insisted on going to his cabin and wouldn't allow nobody to stay with him, not even me.

"I hitched up a wagon of Liefs, put straw in the back fer Ace to lay on, and took him to his home. He had his fiddle close to him, hugging it with his left arm. He must o' suffered terrible pain but he didn't make a sound.

" 'Let me come in and care fer ye, Ace,' I begged.

" 'No, Still,' Ace said. 'I don't live amongst you folks, anymore.' Ace went in his house then, a-weavin' like a drunk man. That made me think of a bottle o' liquor I had in my pocket. I hitched th' team to th' fence and run up th' path, but Ace had closed and barred his door.

" 'Here's some whiskey, Ace,' I called out. 'Let me in, Ace.' But he didn't answer me. So I rode back to Lief's with the team and told him about it. Old Lief died that night, the shock was too much, I reckon, fer Lief was nearly a hundred years old.

"Months went by and nobody saw Ace Lemmon, not even a glimpse. Winter come on, the worst winter ever known in th' mountains. A blizzard covered trails and roads three foot deep with snow and, for it all, not a trace of smoke poured from Ace's chimney. Not a sign was about that a livin' soul was there. I know, fer I fixed up some snowpads and covered the three miles from our place to Ace's two or three times a week, carryin' a hunk o' boiled bacon and some corn pones, thinking he might be hungry. Then, one night about five months after the cuttin', I decided to hang around till night, thinkin' if Ace was still there, I'd see him through the winder.

"It was a long wait in that March cold. I slipped back of the cabin and climbed in the loft of Ace's barn. There wasn't a wisp of hay or straw in sight. What happened to Ace's mule, nobody ever knew. When it got good and dark, I crept over to th' cabin and pressed my face to a winder pane. It was darker on th' inside than on the out, so I couldn't see a thing. I started to call out to Ace when

166

that fiddle of his begun to play. It made the hair rise on my neck and chills run up my back. I knew then that Ace was dead and that was his spirit comin' back, just like he said it would. I reached home in a lather but my folks was all in bed and I was glad because I didn't want to talk about it.

"Well, spring come overnight on Knob Ridge that year. Seemed like the thaw and the bloomin' of the dogwood and redbud was all at the same time. The laurel had the biggest and the waxiest leaves I ever saw and that's the first time I noticed or thought much about God. I thought maybe Ace Lemmon might a-been God and we'd killed Him. I remembered Old Preacher sayin' God was comin' back when folks least expected and nobody'd know when. And I remember Preacher sayin' after that life would be hard to live, and it was. There got to be a spell of thievin' on Knob Ridge, the like of which we never knowed. Folks got sick and a lot of 'em died in strange ways. It got so that folks distrusted each other. Old Preacher set out to hold meetin' after meetin' and nobody would go.

"In the spring, Winnie's baby come and it may be hard fer ye to believe but it's so, fer I saw it. That baby jest had one hand, for a stump was on his right jest like Ace's. Folks rode miles to see that baby and when Jud heard about it he got to drinking. His wife up and left him and went over to Lief's folks, stayed with Winnie.

"I tell ye, it was a awful period o' livin' in them days. Families hung close together with nobody else to depend on. Crops failed that year and grub was scarce. Even game in the woods was hard to find and it was always so plentiful before. I was out with my gun, huntin' squirrels one evenin', when I come out in a cleared spot over what we called Glen View. There was a clean drop there of a thousand feet and you could see across a little valley to Crag Mountain. It was almost night and a new moon was comin' up over old Crag. It was a purty sight and I stood there lookin' and wishin' life was like it used to be. I wished Ace was back with his fiddle to make up a song about the moon like he used to make up songs about anything beautiful. All at once, I heard that fiddle, just as plain as if Ace was right beside me. I stood rooted to th' spot and tried to run but I couldn't. Nobody else had talked of hearing that fiddle and it seemed like I was singled out fer punishment fer a crime I hadn't done.

" 'Oh, Ace, don't do this to me. I didn't have nothin' to do with it. I miss ye, Ace. Life ain't the same any more,' I called out.

"And then it got quiet, so quiet I could hear the wind singin' in th' big poplars. I never was so lonesome in my life nor so empty of heart. Looked like there wasn't nothin' to look forward to or to work for anymore. A voice spoke real soft and said, 'Is that you, Still? I'm in th' cave. Come down.'

"A cave at Glen View? Why, nobody ever heard of a cave around there. I stood there, wondering which way to go, when a light appeared right over the edge of that cliff, a pine knot burning and held in a hand.

" 'This way, Still.' Ace spoke, directing me. I clumb down and finally I felt a hand pulling me to an opening in the face of that cliff. Sure enough, it was Ace Lemmon, but this Ace Lemmon was an old man with long white hair and deep lines in his face. I looked at him and all the time

I was cryin' and didn't know it. Ace put his arms around me.

" 'Now, now, Still, you couldn't help it. Don't fear no more. It's what ye don't know that hurts. I'ts th' strange things ye can't understand.'

"I sat down, then, in that little cave and looked around. That pine torch was set in the wall and gave a good light. Water dripped steady and even off in one corner and made a hole in a rock just like a pan. And hanging here and there in that cave I saw hams and sides of meat and jars of fruit and stuff. There was straw fer a pallet and a sheepskin fer a cover. There was a pile o' corn off to the side.

" 'Don't tell nobody what you see, Still,' Ace said. 'You come here and I'll learn ye to play the fiddle, then when I'm gone, you can have it.'

"I stared at Ace, wonderin' how he could learn anybody to play a fiddle now, him with just one hand. And then Ace reached to a ledge, and took hold of that fiddle and laid hisself on the floor of that cave. If I hadn't seen it, I'd never believe it. He took hold of that bow with the toes of his right foot and his leg moved and sawed that bow and that fiddle began to sing. He stopped after a bit and asked me about Winnie's baby. When I told him about that baby having a stump on his right side, Ace looked out the cave opening.

" 'I loved Winnie,' he said.

" 'Did she know it?' I asked him.

" 'I was waitin' fer her to grow up,' he said. "That's why it hurt me so to know about her baby. It ain't mine. Still, I loved Winnie. I wouldn't have harmed her.'

"Ace picked up his fiddle again and played a cradle

169

song, the prettiest song I ever heard. Seemed to me I'd heard them words all my life and yet they was new.

> Rockabye Baby O, Rockabye O,
> The spring winds blowin' E-o E-o,
> Th' fire is burnin' all warm and bright
> Yore Mammy's guardin' ye day and night.
> Rockabye Baby O, Rockabye O,
> Bye, bye, E-o, bye, bye, E-o.

"The way that fiddle sounded off the last of that song was like th' wind a-blowin' on Knob Ridge. It's always been like that ever since, and everybody can hear it, not just me. You can hear it plainest there on Glen View. I ought to know, fer that's where I built my cabin after Ace died. Ye see, he only lived a few months after that. I went back as often as I could get away without being seen and Ace learned me to play his fiddle. One night when I went to the cave, I found him dead on the floor, his fiddle hugged close to his left side. It almost killed me, for I had a closer feelin' to Ace than anybody who ever lived: wife, child or otherwise. Something in me died, too, that night I found Ace gone. I dug a grave in the cave and buried him with his fiddle. He needed it with him jest like he said in that song about goin' to Jordan. I could get me another fiddle, and did.

"After that, Ace Lemmon was always with me. He is more real in spring than any other time. When the spring wind blows, Ace comes back to Knob Ridge and sings that cradle song, sings it to Winnie. Winnie is now an old granny woman. She never married. I reckon Winnie has paid fer her sin in doctorin' and carin' for folks all these years.

"So that's the story of Ace Lemmon and that's why the spring wind on Knob Ridge is like a woman singing to a baby and you can hear th' cradle rockin'."

15

HOMER SPENT A week cutting wood and it was such slow work with an axe he became restless and impatient. Down in the hollow below the cabin, he felled several trees. Then came stripping off the limbs. After that, he used chains to snake the logs up the hill and into Grandma's yard. The mule balked at every turn and Homer swore and used his whip, urging it on.

"Grandma," he said, "I'm going to have to get some pine off the ridge. I'll never get through this way. That hill from th' holler is so steep."

"Why don't you cut dead stuff?" she asked. "It's lighter and ye can pile up more."

"Why, that dead wood burns like paper, Granny, and it don't hold no heat. I'm goin' to lay down a couple of them big hickories fer back logs. As it is, snow is goin' to catch me sure as hell. Wish I'd started sooner."

"Well, honey, you've worked at something ever' day, seems to me. Wish you'd cut me a little stove wood."

"Homer looked around at the logs he had piled in the yard. He felt best not to chop too much until he gathered as many logs as the weather would allow. He raised his axe for a swift downward stroke when his ear caught a noise from the ridge. He stood poised, listening. Voices, shrill and piping, echoed through the hollow. He saw shadows dart here and there through the trees. That was Jurie and th' kids up on th' ridge. He dropped the axe, dusted his clothes, and started up the hill.

"Just a minute, Homer," Grandma called. When Homer stood in his tracks, making no movement to turn back, she walked across the yard to his side. "I know how ye feel, honey, restless and wantin' to see Jurie, and I don't blame ye a bit. But, can't ye wait till th' snow flies? Aaron won't have nothing to tell then."

Homer stood, undecided. He hadn't told Grandma about Aaron seeing him in the barn lot. He was afraid it would give her something else to worry over. He was worried over it himself. A week had gone by and, every day, he expected to see Jed ride into Grandma's yard. He wouldn't go to the valley with Jed without a fight, but there might be some kind of law about a boy running off. Anyhow, it was lonesome around here. He was powerful restless and didn't know why. Grandma was the salt of the earth, but she was getting so quiet these days, lapsing into long silences. Sometimes she talked to herself. He stood digging his toes in the sand, wondering if he should tell about Aaron.

Grandma laid her hand on Homer's shoulder to assure

herself that he was real. Sometimes when Homer was away at work, the big clock hung before her, so plain she could see the two long hands standing together. Once, she caught herself listening for the clock to strike. It frightened her. She could forget these things when she wasn't alone. She tugged at the boy's sleeve now, impelled to warn him for himself as well as for her own need.

"Homer, don't get careless until a snow comes. Then ye can do anything and be safe from Jed. That's Jurie up in my woods now. Supposin' I go up there and send her down to you? Th' kids won't have anything to tell then."

When Homer didn't answer, Grandma added, "I got a surprise for ye, Homer, come in th' house and see."

Grandma spread a colorful shirt over the covers and Homer's eyes lit up with pleasure. "Is that fer me, Granny?" he asked.

"Sure it's fer you. Ain't you my boy now, Homer? Supposin' ye take yourself a wash and comb your hair, then put on this new shirt. Ye won't know yourself in that big mirror. I decided to go up on th' ridge and get me some walnuts. I might see somebody up there and, do you know, Homer, I might forget to take a sack with me."

Homer laughed. "Grandma, ain't nobody in this cove got as much sense as you."

Twenty minutes later, Grandma pulled herself over the ridge top and held to a sapling, breathing heavily. Her heart beat against her ribs like a heavy hammer.

Ellie saw Grandma first and came running through the woods. "It's Grandma! Look, Jurie, it's Grandma!"

Jurie made a seat for her with gunnysacks and Grandma leaned back wearily against a tree.

"Seems like that's too much of a climb for you, Grandma. You should a-waited. We aimed to surprise ye with a sack o' walnuts," Jurie said.

"Is that a fact?" Grandma looked at Jurie and decided that Homer was right. Jurie was almost grown up and her cheeks were red as fire. Her body was hard and strong, for all it was round and womanlike. Jurie was a beaut, her eyes as blue as the sky. Too bad she didn't have a decent dress. Every young girl should have a pretty dress. Homer couldn't find a girl anywhere prettier than Jurie. Trouble was, she was a Biggers.

"How's Ophie?" she asked.

"Not so well, Granny. I reckon ye know Ma's gettin' ready for another young'un?"

"Want to know!" Grandma expressed surprise, pretending she didn't know.

"Yes," Jurie went on, "I don't know what she wants to get herself in that fix again for, and Bertie just a year old. Seems like some folks ain't got a bit o' sense." Jurie leaned over, removed her heavy brogan shoe and, holding it aloft, shook out pebbles and sand.

"When I marry," she said, "I ain't goin' to have a houseful o' kids."

Grandma laughed. "I reckon ye'd better not marry then, honey, for if a woman was ever built to have young'uns, it's you."

A little learning was due Jurie before she and Homer got to courting off in secret places. It was funny that a girl could live right in the middle of loving and birthing and not apply such things to herself.

"I reckon ye know sleepin' with a man gives ye

young'uns, Jurie," Grandma stated.

Jurie tossed her head. "Sure, I know. I ain't slept with no man and I ain't a-goin' to either!"

"Well," Grandma said, "I reckon plenty of women has birthed young'uns that never slept with a man. Sleepin' ain't got much to do with it, anyhow."

Jurie turned to look after the children. Grandma sat there watching her.

"When did you see Homer last, Jurie?" she asked.

"Why, I don't know, must a-been at school last spring. Why, Grandma?"

Grandma leaned over and whispered, "He's at my house now, Jurie. He run off and I'm goin' to keep him all winter, lessen Jed finds out and comes lookin' fer him. Don't ye let on."

When Jurie didn't say anything, Grandma baited her first hook and threw it amid-stream. "Homer said he aimed to get him a wife soon; said he wasn't goin' to leave th' mountain."

Jurie reached over to lace her shoe, not looking up. "I'd like to know how he'll find a wife now, Grandma, me th' only girl left up here."

"That's right," Grandma answered, "you're th' only one left up here."

Jurie looked up, seeing the smile on Grandma's face. "Grandma Weller!" she exclaimed, "you tryin' to tell me Homer thinks I aim to marry him? Why, he ain't nothin' but a runt!"

"Bein' small-sized ain't got nothin' to do with a good man, Jurie. Homer ain't nothin' but a boy now, but he's growin' fast and before winter's over, I wouldn't be surprised if my cookin' don't make a man of him."

Jurie eyed Grandma suspiciously. "You ain't tryin' to make a match between me and Homer, are you?"

"Jurie," Grandma said, "I told Homer he'd better not hook hisself up with one of th' Biggers tribe. I said he'd better go to the valley and find him a real purty girl."

Jurie picked up a dry twig and snapped it between her fingers. She didn't resent Grandma's slur on her pa, because everybody knew how stingy and mean Aaron was. Maybe nobody knew how overbearing he was at home, how he piled the work on her. If it wasn't for Ma and the kids, she might up and run off, just like Homer.

"Grandma," she asked, not looking up, "What does Homer say?"

Grandma pulled herself to her feet and looked down the slope toward her cabin. "Oh, Homer said there wasn't a girl in a thousand miles as purty as Jurie Biggers." Grandma smiled to herself, noting Jurie's expression. "I can't say I think he's right," she added, piling fuel on the fire. Grandma walked over to join the children, calling back, "I left my gunnysack on the back step. What say ye run down and get it, Jurie."

Jurie looked down the ridge, seeing the smoke from Grandma's chimney. Suddenly, she rose to her feet and ran swiftly down the path, touching saplings as she sped through the woods.

Thirty minutes later she joined Grandma, carrying a sack on her arm and wearing a smile on her face. Stepping up close, she whispered, "Grandma, I ain't never seen such a purty house. Why, that carpet's too purty to step on. And Grandma, that big mirror! I never seen myself whole, before." Jurie looked down and fingered her faded cotton dress. "Seems I never thought of such things before."

Grandma rubbed her chin, eyeing Jurie. It took a man's notice to make a woman start thinking about herself. Funny, that with nearly everybody already moved from the mountain she should still find work to do, and this with the youngest of her folks.

"Jurie," she said, "you ain't been over to see me much of late."

"There's always so much to do at home, Grandma. And there's more of late than ever. Seems Pa ain't ever at home anymore. I reckon you know he's goin' around with that Lige Holder?"

"Yes, I know all about that. You wantin' to move to th' valley, Jurie?"

"I ain't thought much about it, Grandma. It seems I don't have time to think. Ma's awful pindlin' now and so is Bertie. Ma is afraid that new baby will come in th' winter and you won't be able to come over."

"Well, you tell Ophie to stop worryin'. Tell her I'll come if I'm alive."

"Grandma, we can't make cow's milk stay on Bertie's stummick. He pukes it up just as fast as he swallers it down."

"Bertie's old enough to eat something besides milk, Jurie. Ye ought to give him eggs and a little green stuff. Ye got plenty of chickens, ain't ye?"

"Pa sells most of th' eggs but I sneak out some once in a while. I don't know who needs them the most, Ma, Hannah, or Bertie. Ma chews fer Bertie but he spits it out and yells all th' time. Pa don't care about any of us, ex-

178

ceptin' Bertie, Grandma."

"Try boilin' cow's milk fer five minutes and let Bertie have it when it's cooled. You might beat up a raw egg in it, too. I got other remedies. You tell Ophie what I said now, Jurie."

"What about Hannah, Grandma? Nobody pays any attention to her but me. She cries in th' night and I have to rub her legs. I reckon that's growin' pains, ain't it?"

"Might be. I got a bottle of tonic that'll help her. Supposin' ye come over tomorrow and get it, Jurie."

I don't reckon I could come tomorrow, Granny. Pa said he was going to kill a hog tomorrow if it was cold enough. I'll have to help."

"I reckon it'll be cold enough," Grandma said. "Th' wind's changin' now. Wouldn't be surprised if sleet ain't in them clouds right this minute."

Grandma turned and hobbled down the ridge path toward home. Every now and then she stopped to rest, holding to a sapling, feeling her heart beat fast. Seemed her head was light as cotton and her body belonging somewhere else. She found it hard to direct her motion, place her feet securely on the ground. She felt disembodied, floating in space.

"Why, it's just like I was standin' off lookin' at myself," she thought.

She found Homer in her back yard, digging holes and setting logs upright. "What in th' world are you a-doin', Homer? Looks like you're buildin' a house or somethin'."

Homer smiled with embarrassment. "I promised Tom I'd build ye a privy, Grandma. I'm goin' to lay planks from th' door so's you won't have to touch the cold ground in winter."

Grandma laughed, then she looked at Homer tenderly. "That's th' nicest comfort anybody could a-thought of, Homer. But maybe you hadn't better waste them logs. Another thing, this extra work might be fer nothin'. Them Government fellers is liable to be along most any time."

Homer wished he could say something to stop her worrying. A thought came to him. "Grandma, I forgot to tell ye something Tom said. Dr. Mayberry told him them Government fellers wasn't goin' to move any old folks off."

Grandma looked suspicious. "That don't sound right, Homer. Ye ain't a-makin' that up?"

"Course not. And ye ought to know they ain't goin' to move you off in the middle of winter." He looked around. "If I just had th' wood cut and all else done, I'd wish fer a six-foot snow and wouldn't care a damn bit."

Grandma laughed and walked over to her old garden, looking for sage. "I reckon you and Jurie made out all right," she called back.

"Oh, me and Jurie understand each other right good. I reckon." Homer set the fourth log upright and stood back to survey and figure. He couldn't afford to make this privy entirely of logs. He needed those logs for wood. Now if he just had some plank boards and something for a roof.

"Grandma," he called out, "I think I'll take a crowbar over and lift th' tin roof off our old chicken house. Then I'll prize planks off th' barn."

"Why, Homer!" Grandma walked back and stood there, shocked. "Supposin' them Government fellers come along and saw ye? They might put ye in jail! Why, that's stealin'!"

"Hell!" Homer exclaimed. "That's our house, ain't it? Besides, th' only Government fellers I've seen is old and fat and with hair as white as a sheet. They couldn't catch nothin'. Shucks, I'll bring anything else I see that's loose. I aim to build another room on your house fer me and Jurie, unless ye got objections, Grandma."

Grandma smiled. She had no objections. Besides, she doubted if she would be here in the spring and it would be spring before Homer could go about building a room or marryin' Jurie. No need, however, to tell the boy this. He seemed happier since seeing Jurie, so let him have his dream and his hope. That's about all he did have.

"Jurie said they was goin' to kill a hog tomorrow. Made me wish fer some fresh meat, Homer. I just found some sage and it got me to thinkin' of sausage. Ye reckon ye could find a wild hog in the woods? Sam Acree always brought me fresh meat in th' fall but I reckon he had to move before it was cold enough to butcher."

Homer leaned against a post, rolling a cigarette. "Granny, I was goin' to surprise ye about a hog. I got one penned up in th' woods back of our house. I left corn fer him th' other day. You think it'll turn winter tonight?"

Grandma laughed. "Homer, ye beat all I ever saw. One thing is sure: you'll make a good husband fer some girl. All that work Jed piled on ye was hard but it made a man of ye just th' same. Yes," she said, looking toward the mountains, "winter's comin' in any day now. I can feel it in my fingers."

16

GRANDMA WAS cutting rags in strips and rolling them into balls for a rug. She stopped every so often to look around her house. The cabin was warm and snug now that Tom had filled in the cracks. If she just had a new kitchen stove, then everything would be just right for winter. The panes in one window shone bright from her scrubbing. There was a little curtain there now, a brown domestic curtain that hung stiff with starch.

It came to Grandma that nothing in the world was worthless. God meant it to be that way, too, and only thriftless people threw things away. Now take this old pair of overalls of Tom's, worn and patched beyond repair, yet they made three balls of strips for her rug. She had a jug of red-elderberry dye. She had some brown dye, too, made of walnut hulls. It was going to be a pretty rug. She would set it in front of her kitchen stove, so it would be warm and soft to stand on.

The old clock on the mantel ticked away and Grandma wasn't aware of it. Her mind was busy with planning. Winter was a long time and it took a lot of grub to last till spring planting. Perhaps her provender wouldn't last the winter. The few scraps left must go to the chickens.

Grandma got to thinking of the big acorns in the hollow below the house. There had been several nights of frost now, and those acorns kept coming to her mind. Everybody knew that hogs fattened on acorns and that's why folks turned them loose in the woods. That's why some of those hogs went wild and multiplied as they did. You couldn't round them up, you just had to shoot them.

Grandma remembered one winter when her pa went to the woods and brought in two bushels of the biggest acorns she ever saw. He roasted them in the ashes and they ate them hot and mealy. Old as she was now, she could remember how tasty they were that winter when the meal gave out and nobody had any to spare. Last winter, Grandma had been forced to eat acorns several times when her food store got low. She had been desperate on more than one occasion. Why, even the chickens took to those roasted acorns like squirrels. Homer would laugh if she suggested that he gather acorns, for Homer was of this new generation and had no idea of the thrift practiced in the old days, the necessity of it if one lived.

Buttoning herself into a sweater and pulling on a stocking cap, she took a basket and limped down the pathway. The air was cold and crisp and she took a long breath, gripped her cane, and looked over at the mountains. The smoky mist was a heavy curtain. It hung before those peaks like a white wall, crawling lower. Going to sleet tonight, sure as the world, she thought. All at once, the air was filled with a humming noise, coming nearer and nearer.

Grandma's heart leaped with joy. Nobody in the mountains had a car and that meant the Government agents were coming to see her about her land. She stood at her open gate, holding to a post for support. Now that the anticipated moment had arrived, she felt weak and afraid.

The car slowed and came to a stop before her. Two men sat in the front seat.

"Is this the Weller place?" one of them asked.

"I reckon ye know right well what place this is." Grandma answered.

A white-haired man nudged the driver who turned off the ignition. Then they both stepped from the car.

"I suppose you are Mrs. Weller?" the older one asked.

"That's right, Mrs. Ethan Weller, but most of th' folks call me Grandma Weller; that is," she added, "what's left of th' folks."

The two men stood there looking at the ridge back of the cabin, then turned to take in the hollow across the road, and Grandma became fearful. Perhaps she had said something to anger them.

"You're one of them Government fellers, ain't ye?" she asked, leaning forward.

"Yes. Grandma. The Government is about ready to take over the Park now and buy up the rest of the land. I came to look things over and make reports. You have no need to worry, for things won't be any different."

Grandma reached for her pipe, busied herself with filling it. This man was a puzzle. He was out to get something from her and she needed all her thinking powers about her. Whether he would answer her questions honestly or not, she didn't know. She had better go slow.

"Funny thing to me, all the folks moving off so fast. I still can't figure the fairness in none of it."

"Well, Grandma, I don't blame you. If the Park Commission had all this to do over again, they might have handled things better with the folks living here in the mountains. They might have saved themselves a lot of trouble."

"But what's it all about, anyhow? How can anybody feel safe if after livin' and ownin' land for over a hundred years and more, the Government comes in and shows rights to take it away from you? Why, I ain't even knowed there is a Government until the past few years. The Government never done nothing for us mountain folks. We've looked after ourselves."

"You've got me there, Grandma. However, if I put it to you right, I imagine you'll agree that for the past twenty years life up here has been anything but what it used to be. Times change and people change with it. Sooner or later, rule and order must come in."

"Then ye want to buy my land fer the Park? Is that it?" she asked.

"Yes, but we must have it appraised first," he answered.

"You mean to tell me I ain't got no right to make a sellin' price myself?" Grandma's voice rose with anger.

"How old are you, Granny?" he asked gently.

"What difference does it make how old I am! This is my land, ain't it? I got a right to sell it, ain't I?"

"I'll tell you what, suppose you make a price and I'll

submit it to the Commission."

"Oh, no ye don't!" Grandma spat out, "you make a offer now and I'll let ye know if it suits me. Ye think I ain't got no sense about tradin'? Another thing! Don't ye go to sendin' fellers up here a-moseyin' around my woods!"

"Why, Grandma! Would you buy a cow unseen? Would you let a man from the valley come up here and sell you a farm without looking it over yourself?"

"I reckon I ain't interested in no farms in that valley. Why, I ain't even goin' to sell, exceptin' I can stay. Better get that in your head once and for all! I ain't movin'!"

"Grandma, don't worry over having to move. You're as safe as you can be. Why, the Park needs you, wouldn't be complete without you."

"What's that?"

"Why, you're the only old settler left in this cove. Is there anyone else around who knows about the old days? I think not. I wish I had time to hear your stories about those old days. That will be of interest to the visitors who will come through. Be interesting to you, too, Grandma."

"Oh, no, it won't." Grandma said, quickly. "Tom Jenkins told me about that. Nobody's a-goin' to run in and out my house, and I ain't goin' to be made a laughin' stock, neither. Them valley folks'll run plumb over ye if ye let 'em. Let's get this straight now."

The man smiled, appreciating the stories he had heard about Grandma Weller. He knew full well that her cabin would be a landmark long after she was dead and gone. They should be thinking of ways to preserve the traditions around this bit of land. Yet, the picture would not be complete without the old woman. He wished she had more years ahead of her.

"I'll tell you what, Grandma," he said. "You stop worrying now and get your mind at rest. You will never be moved from your home. And, as to the land, we won't get around to buying it until spring."

Grandma leaned against the gatepost for support. The last and remaining question had been answered and it was just as she had feared. Spring was an eternity away. What did Grampy Stillwater say about spring? "Like a cradle rockin'." She felt her heart beat hard against her ribs.

"You all right, Grandma?" The man stepped to her side and looked down upon her anxiously. The old woman's eyes were half closed and her skin like old parchment.

She opened her eyes, then, and pinned them upon the man before her, her mind groping feebly for the lost thread.

"I guess," she whispered hoarsely, "you mean by spring I won't be here and you'll get my land for nothin'?"

"No, no, Grandma. Let's go to the porch, so you can sit down and I'll try to explain it to you."

When she was settled in her rocker, the man sat on the steps, facing her.

"Maybe you can give me part of the money now while I need it," she suggested.

"Listen, Grandma. This is how things are. This Park has cost millions of dollars and not all the land has been bought yet. The States of Tennessee and North Carolina furnished so much money to buy land. The federal Government promised they would come in now and buy up the rest. At present, they are passing a law to set aside the money needed. They won't have that money until spring.

I promise you that the Government won't cheat you. You believe me, don't you?"

Grandma rose from her chair and walked to her door, turned and faced him.

"No, I don't believe you. There's been money to buy other folks' land. Now go on off. I got no more to say."

She walked through her door and closed it behind her, seated herself by the fireplace. She heard the car move down the road. She looked up at the old clock on the mantel. It was ticking away and the hands moved. She wondered how much time was left for her.

After a time she heard the wagon in the yard and, walking through the kitchen, she opened the back door.

Homer stood by the wagon, waiting for her to express pleasure over his findings. He had the tin roof off Sam Acree's privy, two doors, a dozen planks he had prized off the barn, ten bushels of corn, nails, hinges, and a number of other useful items.

"Where did you get that, Homer?" she asked.

"At Sam Acree's, Grandma, and I can't figure why he left some of this stuff."

"Sam meant to come back, else he wouldn't have left anything."

"Come back? Why, Grandma, he took the money and moved off. They won't let him come back."

"Well, Homer, I reckon Sam hated to leave the mountain more than any of the rest, and so far as I can figure out, them Government men change around until they don't know one day what they'll do the next. First they bought land outright and moved people off. Then along come some more fellers who give money and let the folks stay on. No tellin' what they'll do next. It wouldn't surprise me a bit if they decide the papers ain't worth nothin' and the land belongs to the Government in the first place." Grandma leaned against the wagon and gazed at the Chimneys.

"I reckon them peaks could tell many a tale of years gone by," she said huskily. "When I get to feeling unsettled, I just walk out and take a look at the Chimneys. They been there always and always they'll stay, no matter what. Seems like I get a dependence like in the Bible.

"Homer," she went on, "best you stay with th' mountains. Valley ways are strange and wicked and full of temptations to them born away from it. Put your dependence in th' hills and they won't fail ye. This is your home and your land."

Homer fumbled the reins in his hands and looked down at his feet. Tenderness flooded Grandma's heart. Here was the only one of her people who had stayed by her. There was still work for her to do. Strange about that, for she had so short a time left. She must make use of this time for Homer.

"Grandma," Homer said, "I ain't got a thing save what's on my back; nothing but these two hands to work for me. If I marry Jurie, I'll have to work somewhere." The look in her eyes made him add, "Oh, don't ye worry none, Granny. I ain't goin' to leave you as long as you need me. I'm grateful you let me stay on account of Jurie." Homer looked toward the mountains. "Granny, I been thinkin'; seems I never was happy before this and seems like ever' day that comes up here is storin' up somethin' for another time. I don't understand it very good, lessen it's you and the way you make me feel about things. I never done any thinkin' before. Seems like I didn't have no time to think, on account of working, and no matter how much I worked, nothin' come of it."

"Well, honey," Grandma answered, "life's like that everywhere. When ye get as old as me you put all your days in one hand and weigh what they brought ye in the other and, all at once, unless you're spirited and strong, ye forget it's God ye have left. He won't fail ye. I don't believe in preachin' and rarin' round a pulpit and layin' down on th' floor moanin' over your sins. I never took no stock in the churchin' up here. It's ever'-day livin' that counts; rightful dealin' with your neighbors. That's hard enough without gettin' spells of religion off and on, then sinkin' back to the same old ways until another preacher comes to wake ye up again."

"Grandma, are ye tryin' to tell me it's stealin' fer me to take this stuff from Sam Acree's?"

Grandma adjusted her shawl and smiled at Homer.

"Everybody has to do what they think is right, honey. But now you got that stuff here, I wouldn't be surprised if it ain't best to store it. Supposin' ye put it in the crib and then come on to your dinner."

"I'm goin' to fill th' kettle full of water tonight and have it ready fer that hog tomorrow. Ye reckon it's cold enough, Granny?"

"Plenty cold," Grandma answered. "There'll be a freeze tonight."

17

WHEN HOMER drove into the yard next morning with the hog, Grandma was standing by the kettle of boiling water, still feeding the fire. Homer drew in the reins and stood there in the wagon bed, thinking that never had Grandma looked so old and bent, so weak and puny. The ground was frozen hard and the wind was sharp and biting. Unhitching the mule, he took it to the barn, then walked back to the yard.

"Granny," he said, "this is goin' to be too much fer you. Maybe I better go get Jurie to help me with th' butcherin'."

"You'll do nothin' of th' kind," she said, limping to the wagon and peering over the side. "Lawsy, he shore is a big 'un, ain't he? I ain't had a hawg killed on th' place in I can't tell when. I can't wait to get th' lard goin' in that kettle. I got my grinder all ready for th' sausage, too. We'll have us some fried shoulder meat fer supper."

"Sounds good," Homer said. "I reckon I'm goin' to have to kill him here in th' wagon, for all I hate to mess it up. Hell, I don't know just how to manage. Folks always come in to help with butcherin' back at home. Took three men to lift one of them hogs."

"Well, ye got to kill him first, Homer, ye reckon you're stong enough fer that?"

"Hell, that part ain't nothin'. All I got to do is knock him in th' head with that axe and then slit his throat with that knife I whetted on th' grindstone. I tell ye what, Granny. Get th' axe and knife and I'll turn him around so's his head can hang over the wagon bed. Then I'll have to tote that boilin' water in buckets and souse him fer scrapin'."

"But what about turnin' him over and scrapin' on the other side?" Grandma asked.

Homer laughed. "I don't reckon another hawg was ever butchered like this 'un. As fer turnin' him, I'll use a crowbar if nothin' else works."

With all her puttering around, Grandma was soon so worn and weary, she fell to the back steps, able now only to watch.

"Grandma," Homer called out, laughing. "Look at that blood all over your apron. Looks like you killed somebody shore as th' world."

"I wish Jurie was over here to help. Looks like I ain't got no strength any more," Grandma said.

Homer was weary himself. With both hands on the butcher knife, he scraped at the hair, washing it off with pails of water. Time and again he made trips to the spring.

The ground around the wagon was sticky with blood, the messiest job of butchering Homer ever saw and it seemed unending.

"Listen here, Granny. You go in th' house and rest fer a spell. I done this job so many times it don't mean nothin' to me. I can render the lard and cut up the meat for sausage tomorrow."

Grandma rose. "Well, I reckon a little nappin' by th' fire might help, but you get that tub under him when ye slit him open, Homer. And don't ye go to bein' wasteful and throwin' nothin' away. I'll take care of them chitlins' tomorrow."

"Good Gawd, Grandma! Ye ain't goin' to eat th' guts, are you?"

"You've eat worse things and didn't know it, Homer. Anyhow, I have to use them guts to put th' sausage in. Do what I say now."

Homer made a bench against the house wall with planks set on logs. When the hog was fully cleaned, even to entrails and other organs pulled into the tub on the ground below, he sloshed buckets of water right and left, then reached for the axe. Severing the ribs on either side, he lifted out the long backbone and laid it on the bench. Slashing and cutting away, he raised his voice in what he felt was the song of his heart.

> Oh, my gal she is a-waitin'
> Till I grow to be a man,
> So I eat and sleep and work like hell
> To grow as fast as I can,
> Oh de-lay-e-o . . . Oh de-lay-e-o. . . .

"That's about th' worse singin' I ever heard, Homer."

Homer looked up to see Jurie standing at the house corner, a sack of sausage in her hand. She laughed, no compas-
sion for the red that mounted to Homer's hair, his confu-
sion that let the knife drop from his hands.

"Ma sent some sausage over to Grandma. We didn't
know she had a hawg."

Homer picked up the knife, smiling at Jurie. "Shucks!
That ain't th' reason you come over here."

"What did I come fer then?" she asked suspiciously.

"Oh," Homer said airily, "I reckon you just come to see
me."

Jurie swelled. "Of all th' downright gall! I never seen a
man yet that didn't think he owned the roost and all th'
chickens to boot." Homer still smiled, saying nothing.
Funny, but he wasn't tired any more.

"Who you singin' about in them lines exceptin' me, I'd
like to know?" Jurie asked.

Grandma stood in the doorway. "Come off that, you
two! Just like kids a-fussin'. I sure am glad you come,
Jurie. Reckon you got time to help Homer with th' meat?"

"I might stay a hour, Grandma. I don't want Pa to come
home and find me over here. He's gone over to Pine Ridge
to see Lige Holder. Ma told me to hurry back. She said no
tellin' but what Pa would be tanked up with whiskey and
mean as a snake. Makes me so mad. All he does is passin'
back and forth a-jawin' about what he'll do about sellin'. I
don't no more believe Pa aims to leave th' mountain than
nothin'."

Jurie reached for the apron Grandma held out and
picked up a knife to join Homer at the meat bench. Her

strong and experienced hands flew, making quick work of the trimmings for sausage, throwing aside the ribs for Homer to crack with the hatchet. Grandma sat on the step to watch.

"Jurie," she asked, "any of them meetin's ever held at your house?"

"Last week, they sat around for days talkin' and drinkin'. It kept me and Ma at the stove, cookin' fer 'em. Ma said it don't amount to a thing, just talkin'."

"What do they say, Jurie?"

"Oh, there was a man from th' valley leadin' 'em on. Seems like he bought some land a year or so back and now he's mad because they won't give him what he says is a fair price. He told Pa five thousand wasn't near what our place is worth, said fer him to go to court before sellin' fer less than six."

Grandma sat up, interested. "You mean them Government fellers offered Aaron five thousand fer his place?" she asked.

"Yes, they did, and Pa thinks he has to do what Lige says."

So th' Government had money to offer Aaron, Grandma thought. That was queer. Then she thought about Bud Latham.

"Listen, Jurie. What about Bud? They offered him a price yet?"

"Grandma, that old Bud is just a sight. They ain't come around to him yet about his land but Bud don't stay home long enough for anybody to catch him. He just sets off drinkin' whiskey and listenin' to what th' men say and ever' once in awhile, he says, 'Amen!'"

195

Homer was watching Jurie. He had laid down his knife and hatchet and was leaning against the bench, watching her every movement. Gee, she was pretty! Everything around today was so full of living. Seemed Jurie just belonged over here.

"Aaron is a fool," Grandma said. "And it's th' first time I ever knowed him to listen to anybody else. With a family like his, he's lettin' that Lige Holder turn his head. Why, Aaron will be beat out of some of that land money. Tom Jenkins said that's what happened if ye went to court. In th' first place, Aaron's land ain't worth five thousand dollars."

"It's on account of th' gristmill, Grandma," Jurie said. "But Ma thinks just like you do. She and Pa fusses all th' time now, and Pa takes it out on us. It's got so I'm just scared to see him comin' home after one of them meetin's."

Something boiled up in Homer. "You mean Aaron beats you, Jurie?"

"Shucks, Homer. I reckon Pa has wore out a dozen whips on me and it's all on account of me takin' up fer the kids. I reckon I'll learn sometime but I can't see him imposin' on Hannah. She's so little and pindlin'. If that next baby is a girl, Grandma, there won't be any livin' in the house with Pa. I reckon I'll have to run off with th' whole shootin' match."

Homer picked up a bucket and headed toward the spring. "Ye won't have to run far, Jurie," he called back.

Jurie stared after him, then turned to Grandma. "What's he mean by saying I won't have to run far?"

"I reckon," she answered, "that's Homer's way of askin'

ye to marry him, Jurie. Ye could do worse, for all I hope ye don't bring that passel of young'uns over here when ye run off."

Jurie laughed. "Well, I ain't run off yet. I couldn't, anyhow, with Ma gettin' ready fer another baby. It's Hannah I'm worried about, Grandma. She's so scared of Pa she throws up everything she eats. That's why she's porely. Maudie takes care of herself by hidin' off all th' time and that Ellie ain't scared of the devil. Where ye want me to put this meat, Grandma?"

"Oh, drop it in that barrel over there, Jurie. Homer has to salt it down. Leave out a shoulder. I aim to fry some fer supper. Want to eat with us? I got a huckleberry pie and some green-tomato pickle."

Jurie wiped her hands on her apron, looked around the yard, and then back to Grandma. "Gee, Granny, it's so peaceful over here. I got to go now and I wish I didn't."

Homer walked up with the buckets of water. "Say, Jurie, you ought to see th' squirrels up in th' woods. They're feeding on hickory nuts. Let's take a gun up there tomorrow and get us some."

"I'd sure like to, Homer, but Pa lays out so much work when he goes off, I catch it when it's not done. Best you not depend on me. I got to go now, Grandma."

"Help me in th' kitchen with this barrel first, Jurie. Then I'll walk part way home with ye," Homer said.

"Ain't ye goin' on to makin' th' lard and all?" she asked.

"Not till tomorrow," Grandma spoke quickly. "This boy's been up since before daylight, Jurie, and he deserves a rest."

Through the kitchen window, Grandma watched them

climb the trail and disappear over the ridge through the woods. When you're young, she thought, you can't take anything in life seriously. You can't believe trouble is lasting, because the strength that lies in your veins gives you courage to meet what comes, and you find the end all the better for the fight and struggle.

Things now, however, were easier than what they once were. All in all, Grandma would not trade her youth for present times. No matter how old you got, you still had your memories and it seemed to her of late that her childhood was only yesterday.

Standing in her back door, she stood there seeing the sun setting behind the Chimneys. Strong and majestic they seemed to her, real and eternal.

"I will lift up mine eyes unto the hills from whence cometh my help," she whispered.

18

ENTERING THE privacy of the woods, Homer reached over and took Jurie's hand. She walked along with him making no protest, for all she glanced nervously around, hating herself for feeling shameful.

Homer felt this reaction. Stopping in the path, he took her other hand, facing her.

"Jurie," he said, "it may be ye don't look on me as bein' a man, and, standing beside Aaron and Tom, I reckon I never will be of a size. But I'm strong, Jurie. I reckon no other girl ever made me feel like you do. Shucks, I even think about ye after I go to bed at night."

"Homer!" Jurie pulled her hands free and backed against a tree.

Homer stared, wondering what he had said to offend her. All at once, realization came over him and he blushed.

"My Gawd, Jurie! You're just like Grandma, seein' evil

in words where no evil is meant. Don't ye know loving ain't no sin? Don't ye know it makes ye want to get close and protectin'?"

"I reckon that's about all a man thinks about, Homer. I seen enough with Pa and Ophie to know that's all a man wants of a woman. I've been thinkin' a lot about that lately."

Homer squatted to the ground, picked up a stick, and began making patterns in the sand.

"Jurie, Grandma said when a man got old enough, God put a urge in him and after that he started lookin' fer a woman. She said when he found one and knew she was the one he wanted to work fer all his life, then that was lovin'."

Rising, he stepped over and laid his hand on Jurie's shoulder. She drew back quickly and his hand trailed down over her breast, full and rounded. A tremor went over him and his hands clenched.

"Jurie." Homer's voice trembled. "I don't just know how to court a woman 'cause I never loved one before. It may be words to say I don't know or think. It maybe somethin' I ain't done fer all I try to show how I feel. I love ye, Jurie. Why, I'd kill a man who so much as touched ye! That's why Aaron's beatin' ye hits me so hard. Let's run off." He reached for her hand and tried to draw her close. "Let's run off, now," he pleaded.

Jurie pushed against him, battling with herself. There had come to her all at once an answer to the questions bothering her, an understanding of the emotions that tore at her heart and breast, surging to such heights at times she wept in her pillows, restless and unhappy. This, she thought now, was the urge Grandma had talked about. In her case, it drove her to work hard and long for some release, for all she could never find it.

When a soft smile played over her face and a tenderness shone in her eyes, Homer could contain himself no longer. Grabbing her in his arms roughly, he pressed his mouth upon her open lips. For a moment she appeared to yield, for all her strength gave way to the warmth that swept over her body and tingled into her shoes. Then an awareness came to her and she pushed against him with such violence he fell to the ground. He lay there, staring up at her foolishly.

Jurie stood with her arms folded over her breasts, pressing hard against the fast beating of her heart, afraid of the emotion that shook her.

"If you ever do that again, Homer Simmons, I'll knock hell out of ye!"

Homer stumbled to his feet. "I reckon it pleases me enough knowing no other man has made ye know yourself, Jurie. I ain't never felt this way, either. I'll be waitin' around and when ye say th' word, we'll run off and get married."

"Why, Homer Simmons, if you run off and leave old Grandma after what she's done fer you, I wouldn't put no dependence in ye a-tall!"

"Don't go makin' excuses, Jurie. Don't take but a day to get married and Grandma won't mind bein' by herself that long. And remember, Aaron can't do a thing once you're married. It ain't far over to your house if Ophie needs ye."

Jurie turned and walked down the trail, calling back, "I ain't trustin' myself squirrel huntin' in th' woods with you,

Homer Simmons."

Homer ran up and joined her again. "Look, Jurie, don't let me keep ye from comin' to Grandma's. I can't help lovin' ye, can I? But, if ye don't want me close, then I won't. I thought maybe you'd help Grandma with th' sausage while I cut wood. It's awful hard, Jurie, just with a axe. Can't ye come tomorrow?"

"Maybe," she called back.

Homer stood in the path until Jurie was out of sight, then he threw back his head and laughed lustily. Funny how he'd worried about courting a girl. Why, there wasn't nothin' to it a-tall. Grandma was right; a woman did have nature just like a man, only it was a woman's way to be sorter shy and slow. He'd be more careful from now on.

Breaking into a run, he left the protection of the woods and entered the cleared space back of Grandma's cabin. A wind, keen and biting, struck his face and he looked toward the mountains across the hollow. It was snowing up there; every peak showed white. A couple of days and it would reach this cove and he didn't have enough wood cut. He wished now he had left that hog for another time. A whole day of work and it wasn't finished yet. Stepping into the kitchen for the milk pail, he found Grandma standing over the range, stirring fat in an iron kettle.

"Gosh A'mighty, Grandma! You still at that hawg business? You ought to be in bed. I can do it tomorrow."

"No ye won't, Homer. Tomorrow is for wood and don't be botherin' about this lard. I'm just boiling out a bit of grease to make some cracklin's. I been hankerin' fer some cracklin' bread. You like it?"

"Sure I do. I like everything ye cook, Grandma."

Grandma turned, smiling. "You looked at yourself in that big lookin' glass lately?" she asked.

Homer turned at the door, holding the milk pail. "No, why?"

"I reckon you're lookin' more of a man ever day, gettin' taller and fillin' out here and there."

"Gee!" Homer ran across the barn lot, swinging the milk bucket.

Next morning, he rose from the table, smiling over yesterday. "You think Jurie would make a good wife, Grandma?" he asked.

"Wouldn't do no good what I thought, feelin' as you do about her, Homer. A man in love ain't got no sense, blind as a bat. A woman in love is worse. The stronger her feelings, the less her strength against it. I just don't know about Jurie. She's a Biggers."

"Well," he said, reaching for his cap and opening the door, "she won't be a Biggers long."

Grandma sat on at the table, having no strength nor will to do otherwise. Not in a long time had she done such work as yesterday. That was a mistake, she should be saving herself. Queer, these spells she was having.

She came to herself with a start and rose to gather the dishes. The door opened suddenly and Jurie ran in.

"Grandma, Ma's havin' pains and Pa didn't come home last night from Lige Holder's. I'm awful scared, Grandma. Reckon you could come over? Pa's got th' team and I had to come on foot, and I run th' whole way."

"How many months is Ophie?" Grandma asked.

"She says seven but she might be wrong and, anyhow, she likely worked too hard on th' butcherin'. She said tell ye th' water's done broke."

That last remark galvanized Grandma to action and made her forget the strange feeling of weakness. "Run quick, Jurie. Call Homer off th' ridge and tell him to hitch up!" she ordered.

Jurie flew through the door and Grandma began to gather her bags and bottles. She fumbled in her haste to dress, choosing the warm new stockings and shoes the doctor had brought her, buttoning the sweater close to her throat. On top of the coat she put the rain cape, then her woolen cap.

"Grandma," Jurie said, laughing, "it ain't that cold. Why, ye look plumb stuffed!"

Grandma didn't answer. She climbed into the wagon and looked back at Homer, who stood on the porch smiling up at Jurie.

"If I ain't back by dark, Homer, come after me. I don't want no fussin' with Aaron if he turns up."

Homer nodded and Jurie drove through the gate and whipped the mule to a trot. Grandma pulled herself into her wrappings until only her small wizened eyes peeped out. "Sleet in them clouds," she said in a muffled voice. "Winter's comin' early this year and it'll be th' worst one you ever seen." She glanced up at Jurie, who was wearing one of Aaron's old hats turned up in front, a ragged coat open and blowing in the wind. Yep, Jurie was beautiful.

"Grandma, any way of tellin' if that baby is a boy?" Jurie asked.

"Not till ye see it," Grandma answered. "Makes me think of Homer when Effie was born. He was a little tad about six, I reckon. When I was leavin', he run out to the wagon and asked me did I know they had a new baby. 'Is it a boy or a girl?' I asked.

" 'I don't know,' Homer yelled. 'I didn't see nothin' but its head.' "

When Jurie drove on, solemn and unsmiling, Grandma continued. "Ye look just like your pa now, Jurie. I never saw Aaron laugh over nothing. Why, his smile is so crooked it's made a mean line in his face."

"I ain't got no quarrel with anybody over Pa, Grandma."

"Then, for Gowd's sake, let him be a lesson to ye, Jurie. Stop actin' like somethin' without feelings. You got spirit, but your pa's got ye in a harness. How long ye aim to let him drive ye?" Jurie made no reply as she turned the team into the yard and brought the wagon to a stop by the back door.

Maudie ran out to meet them, white and shaken. "Ma's dead," she said. "She gave a yell and then laid down. She won't say nothin'."

Jurie helped Grandma to the ground. Tying the mule to the side fence, she ran into the house, calling to Maudie.

"Keep Bertie in the kitchen, Maudie, and stuff that stove till it roars!"

Grandma walked into the house and found the other children sitting around the bed, pale and solemn.

"Ma's dead, Grandma," Hannah said, her lip trembling.

"No, your ma ain't dead. honey. Take the two little 'uns upstairs and get in bed till I call ye."

"I don't wanta go," Ellie yelled. "I aim to see th' baby come."

Jurie laid hands on Ellie and spanked her up the loft

205

steps. Then she closed and locked the door against her cries of rage. The next hour ushered Jurie into the gruesome realization of life's greatest secret.

"Nothin' to worry over now, Ophie," Grandma said later. "Here, drink this hot toddy and go to sleep." Grandma reeled drunkenly against the headboard.

"Is it a boy?" Ophie asked weakly.

Grandma hesitated, then decided the truth was best. "The baby was a boy but it was born dead. I wish I could a-helped ye give this son to Aaron. You've been workin' too hard, Ophie, and it's Aaron's fault. This is God's punishment on him, running around doin' injustice to people and payin' no mind to his family. Maybe it'll learn him a lesson." Grandma pulled the covers around Ophie's shoulders, then turned and limped toward the fire. "Get me some hot water and some sugar, Jurie."

In the kitchen Maudie sat by the stove holding Bertie in her small arms.

"Is it over, Jurie?" Maudie asked. "I think I'll go out and sit in th' hayloft."

"You'll do no such thing, Maudie Biggers! Your days of hidin' off is over. Hand Bertie to Grandma. If anything happens to him, Pa'll kill ever' one of us."

Grandma sat sipping her toddy, gazing down on Bertie reflectively. "Heat a cup of morning's milk and hand me that whiskey bottle, Jurie," she said, finally.

"Why, Grandma!"

"Do as I say and stop standin' there lookin' like a ninny!"

Grandma lifted Bertie to her lap and with a spoon began to feed him what she called upholstered milk. Bertie grabbed at the spoon and almost overturned the cup.

"Look at the pore little thing. Starved plumb to death, Jurie. That's all in th' world that's wrong with this young'un. See th' color comin' in his face?"

Jurie walked over and opened the loft door and the three young ones crept quietly into the room.

"Maudie," Jurie directed, "take th' kids to th' barn and hunt th' eggs." Hannah hung back and Jurie leaned over and whispered to Grandma.

"Shore," Grandma answered. "It can't hurt her. Come here, Hannah, and get some of Grandma's good tonic. It'll make ye grow strong, like Maudie."

A silence fell on the room suddenly and Grandma looked up to see Aaron standing in the doorway. "What's goin' on around here?" he demanded. Grandma handed Bertie to Jurie and limped across the floor. At that moment Aaron saw Ophie in bed.

"Oh, it's come. It's a boy, ain't it?" The look on Aaron's face was the only soft expression Grandma had ever seen there. She stood looking at him in pity and the words she meant to say did not come.

"It was a boy, Aaron, but it was borned dead. I sure am sorry, 'cause it's th' last baby I'll ever bring."

Aaron turned to Grandma and his happy look turned to grief and disappointment.

"You almost lost Ophie, too, Aaron," Grandma went on. "You'll lose her yet if ye don't take better care of her."

Anger flooded Aaron's face now and the look he gave Grandma was calculating and suspicious.

"Funny thing to me you can bring Jed's kids all right. I reckon you didn't half try. I reckon you're glad," he accused.

"You never have thought about anybody exceptin' your-self, Aaron Biggers. If you'd stayed home where ye belong, did th' hard work you left Ophie, that baby could a-been borned alive. It's your fault, so don't go blaming nobody else."

"Shut up!" Aaron shouted. Pushing Grandma roughly aside, he walked over to the bed. Ophie moaned and Bertie awakened with a scream. Hannah ran to the back door and Maudie scampered up the steps to the loft.

Jurie looked down at two-year-old Mona, clutching at her skirts, then over to Grandma who stood in the middle of the floor, her hand trembling violently on her cane.

"Get your wraps, Grandma, and I'll take you home," she said.

"You'll do no such thing," Aaron yelled. "Let her drive her own stolen mule and her own stolen wagon. She hates me, always has. She done this a-purpose."

Grandma whispered to Jurie. "Give your ma another toddy and spike it strong. Don't worry over me, I hear Homer in the yard." Grandma slipped through the door and closed it quietly behind her.

"You don't look so strong, Grandma," Homer said, when he drove her into her yard. "Wait and let me help ye down." Jumping to the ground, Homer reached up and lifted Grandma from the wagon seat and stood there hold-ing her in his arms.

"Why, Granny, you're jest as little as Effie; don't weigh nothin' a-tall." Walking up the steps and into the cabin, Homer deposited Grandma on her brass bed.

"Want I should take off your shoes and pull th' covers

back?" he asked, worried. She didn't even seem to hear what he said. When she lay back on the pillows, he removed her shoes, then, turning her gently, he pulled off the coat and rain cape and threw the quilt over her. He stood by the bed anxiously. Perhaps he shouldn't leave her but he must get to that wood while he could. There was a moisture in the air, a promise of sleet and snow. By tomorrow that trail to the ridge might be slick as glass and to get that old mule up and down would be impossible. Those logs out in the yard wouldn't last two weeks and Grandma had said that when winter struck, it would hold without breaking.

He leaned over the bed and tugged at her sleeve. "Want me to heat ye some coffee?" he whispered.

Grandma stirred. "Get me a cup of whiskey from that jug on th' shelf, Homer. Then hand me one of them pink pills Doc Mayberry left. I'm just tired and I reckon a bit of sleep will fix me up. Don't worry, honey."

Opening the back door later, Homer reached for the axe and sped up the slope to the ridge. He shivered in his thin overalls and jumper. Once he stopped and looked over in the direction of the Biggers farm. "Jurie," he whispered.

His axe rang out in the woods, and choosing pines and oaks of a foot thickness and because they would be of a size easier to handle, he laid them to the ground with a number of strokes unbelievable in a boy of his apparent strength. Stripping off the limbs was the part he hated most. When he had a goodly amount on hand, he decided to get the mule and drag what he could down to Grandma's yard. As he started down the trail, a fine drizzle hit his face and his spirit fell. If it only didn't sleet. If it would just rain instead and not crust the ground, he'd be able to get those logs off that ridge in no time.

The old mule balked, realizing what the chains meant, but Homer was in no mood for persuasion. He beat and urged it on, one trip after another until the last of his cut logs lay in Grandma's yard. Although night was near he didn't stop.

I'll go back and lay down one of them big hickories, he thought. By mornin', the mule will be fresh to drag it. Old Bess lowed as Homer led the mule into the barn. Throwing down corn and hay for both animals, he made for the ridge trail on a run. He was frightened. He could not remember a single day at Grandma's when he hadn't worked the entire daylight. He should have remembered that wood could not be left to the last. The rain had turned to a fine flying snow and that was a bad sign.

Homer chose a tall hickory nearest home and sunk his axe deep. The chips flew and perhaps because each stroke brought from him a grunt in exertion, he did not hear the man approach.

"Hey! Don't you know it's against the rules to cut that live timber? Plenty of dead stuff around these woods without that, buddy," the man said gruffly.

Homer rested his axe on the ground and surveyed the forester. "And what business is it of yourn that a feller cuts his own trees?" he asked angrily.

"So you think this is your woods?" he asked.

"This land belongs to Grandma Weller," Homer answered, "and I work for her. That's th' same thing, ain't it?"

The man turned and without another word started

down the trail toward Grandma's.

Homer ran after him. "Don't ye go down there worryin' old Grandma. She' sick and unsettled in her mind and I ain't goin' to have her bothered." Reaching in his pocket, Homer drew forth a sack of tobacco and started rolling a cigarette.

"Put that down, son," the man ordered. "No smoking in these woods. And as for that rifle I see leaning against a tree back there, don't go to shooting around here, either."

Homer looked at the forester in astonishment, his face red and angry.

"Now let's get this straight, mister: I reckon you take care of th' Park and that's all right by me but this land ain't th' Park now and I have my doubts it ever will be. You're a quarter mile over your boundary, mister, so get goin'!"

The man smiled down at Homer, stepped up to touch the boy's shoulder, admiring his spirit. Homer drew back and raised the axe.

"You're a bantam fighter, kid," he said. "You're the real goods if I ever saw it. If you ever want a job, come over to the station and call for Brownlow. Remember that name, Brownlow."

Homer stood, watching the forester disappear through the woods in the direction of Bud Latham's. He wondered if Bud had sold his land. Well, Grandma must not know this. It would make her sick with worry. Good Gawd! What would a feller want to live up here for if he couldn't cut wood on his land, couldn't smoke, and couldn't hunt game? What sort of livin' was that? Maybe this was the sort of laws them valley people had.

Homer turned back to his tree but night was so near he could not finish the job. When a squirrel barked above him and he saw him scurry tail up and peep from behind the trunk of a beech tree, he raised his rifle and brought him to the ground, taking perverse pleasure in the act, carrying him by the tail, wrapped around his rifle. Grandma might like some stew for breakfast.

Reaching the house, Homer peeped through the window and saw by the firelight that Grandma was still in bed. He stood there leaning against the wall, cold and tired. Snow was falling thickly now and the ground showed white under a thin mantle. Only the moaning of the wind through the trees broke the deep silence around him. There was something ominous in the atmosphere, some dread that pressed next to his chest and made him afraid. Maybe Grandma was dead! If Sam had not taken old Ezra to the valley, he might be sitting there now in the snow, howling. Shivering in his thin clothes, he opened the cabin door and crept to the bed.

"That you, Homer?" Grandma asked hoarsely. Homer's heart turned over in relief. He reached over to pat Grandma's shoulder by way of answer, then he walked over to put wood on the fire.

"Seems you got a sore throat or somethin', Granny," he said. "I better go milk, only I had to get th' lantern. I stayed on th' ridge as long as I could see to chop."

"I already done th' milkin', Homer."

"Grandma! Ain't you got no sense?"

"Never mind that now, Homer. I can't leave everything to a boy like you. It's hard enough as it is. Go eat your supper while it's hot. I made ye some cracklin' bread."

19

Homer sat on the side of the bed tick, pulling on his shoes. Outside, the wind howled around the corners, groaned through the cracks in the cabin, and whistled down the chimney. He placed the last of the logs on the fire, watching the fire blaze high for all it seemed to give out small warmth. He shivered, rubbed his hands together, and looked over the room, indecision on his face. Grandma was still asleep. Her breathing filled the room with dry, rasping sounds.

A month and Homer had seen no one save Grandma. There had been days when he argued to keep her in bed, but for the past week she had made no protest. It was just as Grandma had said, winter came in one night like a lion and it was still roaring on the mountain. He walked over to the bed and stood looking down at her, anxiously.

"Granny," he whispered, "want I should go to th' valley

for Tom and Doc?"

Grandma stirred and her voice was a hoarse whisper. "What's it like outdoors, Homer?"

"Snowstorm, Grandma. Biggest flakes I ever seen. Wind is powerful high and th' whole earth is so white and full of humps you can't tell one thing from another. It's awful purty, Grandma. Want I should pull your bed to th' winder?"

Grandma shook her head. "Heat a cup of water and bring the turpentine, Homer." A fit of coughing took hold and she lay back finally, quiet and exhausted. Fear clutched at Homer's heart. Grandma was worse this morning. Maybe she was going to die like Tom said. He sped to heat the water, bringing not only the turpentine but cough tonic as well. He followed directions and soaked a cloth in the turpentine and lard and slipped it around Grandma's throat as gently as his clumsy, oversized hands would allow. He heated a rock and placed it at her feet. When she continued to shake with a chill, he opened the bureau drawer and lifted out the silk and woolen comforter, spreading it over the bed.

"I was savin' that for you and Jurie," she whispered.

Homer leaned over and kissed the wrinkled cheek. "I reckon that quilt would warm us a lot better, knowing it covered you first, Grandma."

Grandma reached for Homer's hand. "You're a fine boy, honey, near on to bein' a man. You and Tom is th' sort th' mountains used to yield. You won't be sorry helpin' me, Homer. I always show myself grateful one way or another."

Pore Granny. Always thinking of somebody else and nobody ever thinking about her. Love all mixed with pity

214

tore at Homer's heart.

"You talkin' of dyin', Grandma? I never heard of such. Spring is just over th' ridge. Th' sun is a-laughin' at this snow and wind right now. I reckon winter's showin' off with another fling."

"Spring?" Grandma whispered. She meant to remember something about spring. What was it?

"I reckon winter's just started, Homer. I was wonderin' if th' ground would be too hard and the snow too deep."

"Too deep for what, Granny?"

Grandma stirred, looking up in the rafters. Those rafters were naked and empty. She had forgotten her filled kitchen, her wealth of winter provender.

"Homer, I want ye should bury me under th' pine tree next the cellar. That was our store of plenty in th' old days. Sometimes it was near on to bein' empty but Pa never let it get plumb naked of somethin' or other."

Was Granny going to die now? Oh, Gawd, he had to do something!

"Homer, take good care of them acorns behind th' flour barrel. They're real tasty when ye roast 'em in th' ashes."

Homer walked over to the window and looked out. "Grandma, want me to fix ye somethin' to eat?"

"No, I ain't hungry. You fed th' chickens, yet? I reckon Daisy's brood is good-sized fryers by now, ain't they?"

"All the chickens is in the hayloft, Granny. I'm goin' out to feed and milk now. Reckon it's safe to leave ye fer a bit? I might have a rabbit in one of my traps. Rabbit stew might set you up right pert, Grandma." Homer turned and walked back to the bed. He knew he must go after somebody to stay with Grandma while he made an effort to reach Dr. Mayberry. He should have gone sooner.

"It'll be good fer ye to get out, Homer. You got on my woolen stockings like I told ye?" Homer nodded. "Then put on my sweater, too, and take my mittens."

"You'll be all right with me gone?" he answered.

"Don't worry, honey. Don't worry a bit."

Homer patted Grandma's shoulder, then ran from the cabin. He couldn't trust himself to say more. Stepping from the porch, he sank into snow to his knees. Gawd, he had never seen such a winter in the mountains! He glanced at the small mound that was the remnant of his woodpile, wondering over the amount he had cut, the logs that had gone up the chimney in smoke. Being old, Grandma wanted a roaring fire all the time and it sure took plenty. Seemed impossible to have burned that much in so short a time.

Well, he must get some wood somewhere before he could go to the valley for Dr. Mayberry and Tom. This snow was going to keep up all day and to get that old mule up and down that ridge trail was impossible. It would slip and flounder and maybe break a leg. He walked to the barn. After milking old Bess, he set the bucket on a shelf and threw down hay.

"Old feller," he said to the mule. "You've rested long enough around here. Got to pay fer your feed." Driving from the barn on his crudely improvised sled, the mule floundered through the snow across the barn lot and Homer turned it toward the Biggers place. Time and again Homer jumped off to lift a corner of the sled, caught in a snag or lowered into a rut. It was a long trip and he found himself off the road several times, what with the snow so thick he could hardly see three feet ahead of the mule. He pulled up at Aaron's side door with a loud "Hello!"

"What in hell ye doin' out in such weather as this, Homer? Ain't ye got any sense or feelings fer that mule?"

Homer looked at Aaron, standing in his back door. He wished just once he could plant a fist on Aaron's jaw that would lay him as cold as that snow. Some day he'd be big enough.

"Grandma's awful sick, Aaron," he said. "I come over to get Jurie to stay with her while I go fer Doc Mayberry and Tom. I thought you might lend me a little wood till I get back. I might be two days comin' and goin'."

Aaron threw back his head and laughed. "Just as I thought. So Grandma's callin' on me. She ain't as smart as she thinks she is." Aaron lowered his brows to scowl at Homer.

"And you're a fine one, too, Homer. Think you're a man, I reckon. Well, a man would cut enough wood to see him through a winter without beggin' at a feller's door. I got my idees over Jurie goin' over to Grandma's. I know what she's up to. And," he added, walking through the snow to Homer's side and looking down on him with anger shooting from his eyes, "I know what's in yore mind, too, Homer Simmons." Aaron reached for Homer and shook him until the reins dropped to the ground.

"You let Jurie alone! Ye hear me? Any more of such doings and I'll whale th' hide off yore puling body! Ye ain't nothin' but a undersized runt, runnin' off from Jed in winter and spongin' off pore mountain folks. A fine man you'd make for Jurie or any other girl fool enough to marry ye!"

Aaron stepped back and made for his door as Homer reached over for the reins. Feeling in the snow, he touched a small hard object and his hand came up with a stone the size of a cup. With a quick, impulsive movement, he straightened his back and let the rock fly with all the strength he possessed. It caught Aaron a glancing blow on the head and he reeled for a second, then fell face down in the snow. The dogs under the porch yelped and howled and the windows of the kitchen rattled as Ophie and Jurie ran across the floor in alarm.

"Oh, what have ye done, Homer Simmons?" Ophie ran to the yard, stumbling in the snow to reach Aaron's side. Kneeling, she drew his head into her lap.

"You've killed him, that's what you've done!" she wailed.

Jurie was pulling on a coat with rapid fingers. Slipping a stocking cap over her hair, she ran to the yard.

"He's openin' his eyes, Ma. You can't kill nothin' as mean as him. You'd better get in th' house before he comes to." Jurie jumped on the sled and shouted, "Turn around quick, Homer, and drive like hell!"

Standing as white as the snow, his anger cooled, Homer was like a statue, unable to move. Jurie grabbed the reins from his hands, almost turning the sled end up as she pivoted and drove from the yard. She looked back as the mule passed the gatepost and saw Aaron rise to his knees. She had her arms around Homer, holding him up and encircled with the reins.

"Don't worry, Homer. It takes more than a rock to kill Pa. I've wished many a time I could let one fly like that."

Homer reached for the lines. He was in command of

himself now.

"Better sit flat, Jurie. Aaron will follow us with his team and we've got to get a start on him."

The ruts over which he had previously traveled were almost hidden with the falling snow but the old mule traveled as never before, urged and beaten the whole two miles. Pulling up in front of Grandma's cabin, Homer turned to Jurie.

"You won't leave Grandma, no matter what?" he asked.

Jurie shook her head, more fearful of Aaron than she would ever let Homer guess.

Homer stepped up close and took her hand. "Honey, I promised things back on th' ridge and it's hard to keep. Oh, Jurie, I been so lonesome for ye. You don't mind my sayin' it, do ye? I reckon I ought not to be thinkin' of such now, Grandma up there, dyin'. But Grandma knows, Jurie. Grandma understands everything."

Jurie looked through the snow toward the cabin, then turned her eyes down the road toward her home. There was something wild and free about Grandma's place. A person got a feeling somehow that nothing was wrong here. It was just like stepping through walls and coming out into a world that stretched out hands in all directions, inviting you on. Homer was right. When people loved, they did want to get close.

Homer stood there watching Jurie with puzzled and disappointed eyes. A feller got so far in courting a girl and then he was against a wall.

"Jurie," he whispered, "don't ye love me just a little bit?"

Jurie laughed, but her laughter was the bubbling over

of happiness, a new sense of freedom, a freedom she knew now she would never let go. The look she gave Homer was like a flood of tenderness sweeping over him, wiping away all doubt. They reached for each other, standing in close embrace while the falling snow continued to cover them.

Shaken, Homer pushed away finally. "Get in that house, girl. Gawd, Jurie! I could fight a whole army!"

Jurie's laugh echoed back as she plowed through the snow toward the cabin. Homer unhitched the sled, then jumped to the mule's back and headed toward the highway. The snow seemed to get deeper as he approached Bud Latham's place. The old mule foundered and heaved, coming to a full stop in front of Bud's gate.

"Oh, so ye think this is as fer as you'll go, eh?" Homer dug his heels into the mule's flanks and beat it with the reins but the mule stood with head down, stubbornly refusing to go on. Homer looked up at the house, surprised to find no smoke from the chimney. Sitting there in the falling snow, shivering with cold, and knowing now that the old mule would never make it to the highway, he thought of a plan. He would stable the mule in Bud's barn, thaw himself out with a fire in Bud's house, then try to make it on foot to the CCC camp.

He slipped from the mule's back into snow over his knees. The old mule stumbled after Homer into the barn lot. Homer found plenty of corn and hay and dropped down a plentiful amount in the manger.

"I reckon you've earned a rest, old feller," he said, smacking the mule on the rump and closing the stall bar. "As fer me, I've got to go on."

Standing in the barn doorway, Homer looked through the snow to the valley beyond. Bud's house looked out over a wide view of the country below. The space seemed to go on and on without end. Too bad you couldn't just swing over the edge and land in the valley without all that treckin' around.

He thought of Jurie back at Grandma's looking after her needs in ways he could not do. Jurie loved him. Knowing that now, nothing else mattered save that he do what he could for Grandma. Homer didn't want Grandma to die. He thought back now to the days before she took to her bed. She sat by the fire, rocking and smoking and talking to herself. Sometimes when she heard sounds, she walked to the window to look up the road, watching for the Government agents. She talked to her dead husband, Ethan. She told him to go over to them Government fellers and make 'em pay the land money which was their rightful due. She told him to buy her a new kitchen stove and some new dishes with roses on the plates.

Homer started for Bud's house and as he stumbled through the deep snow and pushed his way through the drifts, it came to him that he could not possibly get to the highway and to that camp, much less to the valley. Even if he did, it might take days and Grandma would likely be dead by that time. Aaron might go over and take Jurie off, leaving Granny to die by herself.

Reaching the porch he pulled himself up by holding to a corner post. The post was rotten and gave way under the strain, throwing Homer backward and completely burying him under an avalanche of snow that swept from the sagging roof. He came up fighting and swearing at the top

221

of his voice.

Bud stood in his doorway, bent and haggard, but he could not suppress his humor. "This ain't no time to be a-washin' yourself, Homer." Bud's voice was hoarse and his white face winced with pain as the cold wind chilled him, sending rheumatic twinges through his joints.

Homer shook snow from his clothes, struck his shoes against the house wall, then stumbled through the doorway. Bud limped across the floor, climbed into bed, and pulled the covers around his chin. He lay there eyeing Homer, hopefully.

"I don't know what in Gawd's name I'd a-done if ye hadn't come, Homer," he said.

Homer walked over to the hearth and stood looking at the cold ashes. The corners of the cabin revealed not a chip of wood. A gust of wind swept down the chimney, blowing the ashes over the floor, and the house groaned under the winter's blast.

"How long ye been like this, Bud?" he asked.

"Oh, about a week, I reckon."

"You mean you ain't had a fire and nothin' to eat in all that time?"

"I got wood cut but it's under them drifts. I couldn't risk wadin' in that snow with this rheumatiz. Now, if I jest had me a quart o' whiskey." Bud looked over at Homer, hopefully.

"Grandma says whiskey is what gives ye these spells, Bud. Looks like ye ought to have more sense than to drink it, knowing that."

Homer plunged into the snow again, looking for the woodpile. Bud was right, he did have a good-sized pile. He wished he had some of it at Grandma's. What would Jurie do when she burned the last stick?

With scraps of damp bark, he knelt and tried to kindle a fire. His hands were stiff and blue with cold and the wet ashes made fire-making all the more difficult. The first of his three matches licked up the dry edges of the bark, flickered, then went out. Looking around the house he searched for paper. The place was a complete wreck, filthy and vile-smelling. He told Bud so and then opened the door.

"Shut that door, ye dern fool! Ye want I could catch pumonia?" Bud yelled.

"Hell, you'll catch somethin' worse than that, I'm a thinkin'." Homer said, disgustedly. "Damned if I'll stay in this nasty hole another minute! You get outta that bed and make a fire yourself and then scrub that floor. Grandma's about to die and look at me, over here 'tendin' to a drunken old sot who ain't worth th' powder and lead to shoot him."

Homer laid the two matches on the mantel and started for the door.

"Come back, Homer! Don't leave me like this." Bud was wringing the bedclothes, his voice a whining cry.

Homer stood in the doorway, undecided. He couldn't leave Grandma to die without a doctor seeing her. He didn't see any way possible to get to the valley, but he had to make an effort. He walked back to the bed and stood looking down at Bud.

"I reckon you didn't hear me tell ye that Grandma is up at her place, dyin'. I wouldn't be surprised if she ain't dead already. Bud Latham, you get outta that bed and start thinkin' about somebody else fer a change!"

Homer pulled a calendar from a nail and his second match caught the paper and blazed high for a few seconds. When the flame flickered weakly, he glanced quickly around the house, noting a crumpled mat made of corn shucks. Grabbing it up, he stuffed it near the tiny flame and then chuckled to see the fire take hold and roar up the chimney. Bud lay on the bed, watching.

"You might burn th' table and chairs next, Homer, wouldn't make no difference to me." Bud threw back the covers and reached for his shoes.

"What ye doin'?" Homer asked. "You better stay in bed till this house gets warm." Homer was piling on logs now and the fire was crackling noisily. He pulled up a chair, slipped off his shoes and began to peel the wet stockings from his frozen feet. He draped the sweater over the floor and sat watching the steam rise.

"Bud," he called, "how's the best way to reach that camp? I got to get Doc Mayberry up here. I ain't never talked on a telephone before, so I don't know which way to turn."

"I'll go," Bud said, hoisting his pants as he walked toward the fire. "You go back and stay with Grandma soon's ye get dry." A twinge of pain struck across Bud's face as he leaned to tie his shoe. He shouted loud, "Damn this infernal luck o' mine!"

"You're so dern weak from eatin' no grub, ye couldn't get a mile on foot. I ain't a-trustin' ye a bit. I'll go myself, but one thing you can do, Bud, and that's haul some wood over to Granny's while I'm gone."

"You mean you ain't got no wood in her house? What in

tarnation ye mean lettin' winter come and no firewood! I'm a good mind to whale hell outta you, Homer Simmons."

Homer had had enough. Hadn't he already wasted half an hour on this drunken old fool? Hell, he had worked every single day at Grandma's. He rose, anger all over him. His fist shot out and Bud lay sprawled on the floor.

"You look like tellin' somebody what to do when need comes, makin' promises to Grandma and keepin' none of 'em! Hell and damnation! Ye can't even look after yourself, much less anybody else. I wouldn't depend on ye fer five minutes, Bud Latham." Homer drew on his clothes and Bud raised himself from the floor.

"I'm goin' now," Homer said, making for the door. "If you don't get that wood over to Grandma's while I'm gone, Bud Latham, I'll break your blasted neck, you damned old sot!"

"Wait a minute, Homer." Bud ran to the door. "How am I goin' to get wood over there? I ain't got no mule or nothin'."

"Oh, yes, ye have. He's out in your barn now." Bud stood watching until Homer disappeared around the turn in the road, then he reached for his heaviest clothes.

20

THREE HOURS later Homer reached the highway. The snow was still falling. He looked up and down the road, wishing he had a sled. He could skim down that mountain road and be there in no time with a sled. Standing there undecided, cold now beyond feeling, he found himself listening. There came through the air a chugging sound that was far away, faint and indistinct as it rose over the wind. Surely it wasn't an automobile. Why, a car could never get over the road. But it was a car, or it resembled a car. It was approaching him now with a broad spray of flying snow blowing in all directions. He scrambled through the snow and made his way to the center of the road, waving and gesturing wildly. The contraption stopped and a head appeared through an open window.

"Well, well! If it ain't Santa Claus. Hey fellows, look! It's old Nick."

Two boys from the CCC camp jumped to the ground and made their way to Homer's side.

"What in hell is that?" Homer asked, pointing.

"That's a snowplow, buddy. Where in the world are you going in such weather?"

"I was aimin' to get to th' camp and call Doc Mayberry on account of old Grandma Weller's dyin'."

"Hey!" A voice called out. "Let's get going."

"Come on," the boys invited, "we're on the way to camp now."

Homer climbed into the truck.

"What's this about a doctor, son?" Homer looked up into the face of a captain from the CCC camp. Then he glanced around at the six boys, all dressed alike and in warm woolen clothes. He explained about Grandma.

"And where does Dr. Mayberry live?" the officer asked.

"In the valley," Homer answered.

The boys laughed and the captain shook his head. "Well, don't worry, we'll find him."

Homer was so tired and so cold, he had no strength left to oppose any suggestions. When the truck came to a stop before a building in the camp, the boys piled out and ran in various directions.

Homer followed the captain into a warm room, where several men were sitting around a hot stove.

"Snow is letting up," the captain announced, unwinding a scarf and divesting himself of outer garments. "Found this boy up the road in search of a Dr. Mayberry. He says there's an old woman sick back in Weller cove. Any of you know Dr. Mayberry?"

"Sure," one of the men answered. "All you need to do is

call the Knoxville operator."

The captain walked to the phone and Homer stood there feeling warmth creep into his chilled body, a bit embarrassed by the glances of the men.

"That you, Mayberry? This is Captain Wilburn, CCC camp, Oakmont. You know an old lady named Grandma Weller? You do? There's a boy here named Homer Simmons. We found him on the highway, trying to reach you. Oh, you want to speak to him?" The captain reached out the receiver and Homer walked up, trembling so his hand shook.

"Yes, Doc, it's me all right. You sound just like yourself, Doc. Oh, I reckon it's pumony Grandma's got. She can't hardly breathe and she's so weak I'm afraid she won't last long unless you hurry. You'll come, won't ye, Doc? And listen, I reckon ye might as well bring a coffin 'cause I know she's goin' to die. She said she was goin' to die and Grandma knows everything."

Homer stood holding the receiver long after the line was disconnected. Captain Wilburn took his arm and led him down a corridor.

"First thing, Homer, you've to get some dry clothes. Then you get a hot dinner. After that, we'll take the snow plow and open up that cove road so the doctor's car can get through. What you think of that?"

Homer stood in the shower room in bewilderment. Something was wrong somewhere. Why, this was a wonderful bunch of fellers and, damn it all, they were Government fellers, too.

The door opened and several boys walked in. They peeled off their clothes and stood under running water, washing with soap, even to their heads. Good Gawd! And this is winter; it's a wonder it didn't kill 'em.

"Here you are, Homer. Captain Wilburn said as soon as you washed and changed clothes, he wants to talk to you." Homer took the bundle of clothes and a heavy towel.

He looked down at the warm woolen coat and pants, the heavy pair of shoes hanging over his arm, new shoes like he'd never owned before. He wished he knew how to say he was thankful. The boys drifted out and Homer turned to the washbasin. He threw off his wet clothes and rubbed himself vigorously as he had seen the others do. When he stood fully dressed even to the high-top boots, he was never as proud in his life. If Jurie could only see him now.

21

Jurie sat by the bed wrapped in an old quilt, watching Grandma with troubled eyes. She had never seen anyone die but something told her that Grandma's breath was leaving her, slowly and painfully.

Grandma was somebody who had always been there, taken for granted like the Chimney Tops and the sunrise. When she was unable to dispense her healing as willingly and freely as before, people gathered to call down wrath and anger, imply unkind reasons to all Grandma said and did. They gave her no credit, gratitude for the years that had gone in unpaid obligations; forgetting that except for Grandma some of them wouldn't even be here.

Even I might not be here, Jurie thought. She thought, too, in looking at this wrinkled face before her that surely this old woman could never have been a baby. Might as well think that Little River had once been a wide sea.

As far back as Jurie could remember, Grandma had always looked the same. But you didn't notice changes in people when you lived close to them; you just took things for granted that were near and a part of you. Why, then, should people wear themselves out doing for folks, going on day after day in thankless services? What you did was in some folks' mind no more than what you should do; was even expected of you. What sort of living was that, anyway? Working so hard you were hungry, so you ate three times a day to get strength to work some more. Then, when you were so tired you couldn't work any longer, you went to bed and to sleep, to store up strength to start all over again. Day after day and year after year, and if you lived as long as Grandma had lived, you died finally, cold and alone. No one came to thank you while you lived. Perhaps no one would even come to stand over your wasted strength.

Jurie dropped the quilt and leaned over the bed. "I don't want ye to die, Granny. I ain't never had a chance to do nothin' for ye. Seems this is the first time I even thought about it and it hurts me a lot." Jurie reached for Grandma's hand. "Let me do somethin' for ye, Granny, somethin' to make up for all th' rest. I'll do anything ye say, no matter what."

Grandma smiled. "You ain't all Biggers after all, Jurie. Don't mind my sayin' that. Just remember to keep your spirit always and be kind to them that's weak. Don't expect nothin' of anybody, lessen ye do things fer them. Stand up fer what ye think is right, even if ye stand by yourself and even if it's against your own folks. You understand what I mean?"

231

Jurie nodded, tears gathering fast. "Yes, Grandma, ye mean Homer."

"Then ye love Homer, Jurie?"

"Oh, yes, Granny."

"Honey, ye couldn't find a better boy than Homer if ye looked th' world over. He'll work hisself to death to give ye the best that's in him. He's that kind, Jurie. Be grateful just fer that and never expect more than a man can give. When he's weak, give him some of your own strength and don't never judge him by anybody else." Grandma closed her eyes, speaking low. "Th' blood of th' mountain will go on in you and Homer, in th' children that live after ye. Can ye write, Jurie?"

"Sure, Granny. I been through the fifth grade."

"Then lift that third board near th' winder and bring me them papers." Grandma's breathing was difficult with this exertion. She must hold on a little longer, for there was something she had to do. Ever' so often there was a haze in the room. It was like the smoke on th' mountain.

Jurie walked back to the bed with the land deeds in one hand, a paper and pencil in the other. Grandma reached for the deeds, fondling them in her fingers.

"Write down what I say, Jurie. I take it my right and justice to pass on my land to anybody that suits me." Grandma paused and Jurie wrote these strange words with painstaking efforts, stumbling over the spelling. She wondered what it was all about. Pore Granny, maybe her mind was wandering.

"And I call down th' wrath of Gawd on them that goes against my dying wishes!"

"Grandma! That scares me."

At this point, a noice was heard in the yard. Jurie jumped up and reached for Homer's rifle. Grandma smiled. "That's Aaron, Jurie. Lay down the gun, for ye won't need it. Remember what I said about bein' strong and lettin' folks browbeat ye?"

The door opened with a clatter and Aaron barged in, bringing with him a gust of wind and snow. His face was dark and angry, his swollen eye almost closed. He didn't glance toward the bed. He shook his hat, throwing melted snow onto the covers, advancing toward Jurie.

"Get yore things on, ye little bitch! I'll teach ye a lesson ye won't forget!" Jurie was stepping back as Aaron advanced upon her, trying to find that strength Grandma talked about; it shamed her to feel her heart beating fast with fear.

"Runnin' off in th' woods like a dog! Hidin' around in th' bushes and bein' led on by an old woman who ain't no better than what she ought to be!" he ranted.

Anger filled Jurie to impulsive action. Reaching for a chair, she swung it over her head with the lithe strength her hard work had given her. Aaron threw up his arm to protect himself, unable to do otherwise in his complete surprise. The chair struck and crashed to pieces in Jurie's hands. Standing five feet six and weighing a hundred and twenty-five pounds, Jurie was no match for Aaron. She knew this even as she advanced toward him again, waving the chairback. When he stood, white-faced, his left arm hanging limp and useless, Grandma spoke.

"That's enough, Jurie. Leave him to nurse that broken arm, 'cause there ain't nobody now to give him healin'. Get th' papers, I don't think I'm goin' . . . to last long."

"Look what ye made me do to her," Jurie shouted to Aaron. "If she dies, you killed her, and if ye ever come close to me again, I'll kill ye!"

"You ready to write, Jurie?"

"Yes, Granny."

"To Homer Simmons, I leave my land and my home in his full right and possession, to hold and to keep as long as he lives and as long as his wife lives after him, it shall be her home. Any money comin' from th' Government is to go half to Homer Simmons and half to Tom Jenkins." Grandma stopped for a breath. She must hurry.

"Aaron," she called, "come here and witness this paper. I don't hold anything against ye, Aaron. I just feel sorry for ye and th' heart inside ye, that's so hard and crusty." Grandma raised up and scribbled her name, then directed Aaron to sign under it. She fell back on the pillows, calling, "See th' clock on th' wall, Jurie? Look, it's goin' to strike. Listen."

Jurie followed Grandma's eyes to the side wall, fear and bewilderment in her face. Was this death?

"Oh, Granny, please don't die." She fell to her knees beside the bed, buying her head in the covers. Back on the mantel the old clock was striking—one—two—three . . . twelve. Jurie counted to the end. Then she rose and stood there looking on Grandma's stillness, the look of peace on her face.

Aaron stood at the foot of the bed for a minute, then he turned and closed the door softly behind him.

Jurie felt weak and spent with the emotional strain, the tension of the day. The tears she shed left her clean and dry inside and she stood shorn of all the fears and struggles of childhood: a woman grown and full of understanding. Grandma was dead and what was to be done now was only the custom of decency, for Grandma would not know. Jurie pulled up the blanket, then she turned to tidy up the cabin against the coming of Homer and Dr. Mayberry.

As night came on, the house grew colder. The fire was low on the hearth, for the wood had disappeared long since, even rails from the fence which Jurie pulled across the snow and into the house. Perhaps if she went to the barn, she might find a few stray pieces for the cook stove. Slipping on her coat and cap and reaching for the milk bucket, she pushed through the snow across the barn lot. Old Bess was lowing, and the chickens were clamorous, seeming to sense some ominous change in their surroundings. Jurie shelled corn to throw in the runway for the chickens and dropped four ears for the cow. She made short work of the milking. Holding the full pail in her hand, she looked around. Perhaps she could pull a few boards from the trough. She looked up startled when Bud appeared in the doorway.

"I got here soon's I could, Jurie. I brought some firewood like I promised Homer. Is Grandma all right?"

Wood! It was a comforting word. Jurie stepped ahead of Bud and motioned for him to follow. Bud looked so old and bent, so white and sick, she didn't have the heart to tell him. He would find out for himself. When they stepped into the lean-to, Bud saw the jug of whiskey on the table and his eyes lit up with pleasure. "Gawd, I'm sure glad to see that likker!"

Jurie stopped him with an arm. "Supposin' ye go in and see Grandma, before you try such tricks, Bud." Bud stared for a moment, took off his hat, and shuffled through the door.

Jurie strained the milk and looked around to plan for supper. Even with folks lying dead, those living must eat. After all she had been through, Jurie felt downright disloyal in the pangs of hunger she felt. She had eaten no dinner, what with looking after Grandma's needs and all that followed. Though Grandma was dead, and she was still in her house unburied, those who came to do her final honor should find her table bountiful, an expression of the same generosity Grandma had shown while she lived. This Jurie could do for her and she would.

"Why didn't ye tell me, Jurie. Pore old Grandma." Bud walked over to the table, uncorked the whiskey jug, looking around for a cup.

Perhaps he needed it, Jurie thought. He was drunk half the time, anyway. She handed him a cup and watched him pour it full, gulping it down like water.

"Go get some wood now, Bud," she said. "I got supper to cook. You better build up the fire in the cabin, too, and lay by enough wood fer tonight."

22

WHEN SEVEN o'clock rolled around and no one had come, Jurie and Bud sat down to eat their supper. Bud had fortified himself with swig after swig from the jug and, as always before, the liquor touched his conscience, making him penitent and tearful. He cried into his plate while he swallowed cups of scalding coffee, ham and eggs, and a wedge of Jurie's apple pie.

"I reckon a feller just has to eat, no matter what," he said, wiping his mouth on the sleeve of his dirty shirt. "Things are goin' to be different now."

Things were always going to be different with Bud. Jurie felt sorry for him, no matter his filthy appearance.

"Bud, I'd be downright ashamed to go to Grandma's funeral, nasty as you. Soon's I clean these dishes, you come in here and take a wash."

"Listen," Bud cautioned. Over the wind could be heard

the chugging of a motor. Jurie ran through the cabin and opened the door to Homer, Dr. Mayberry, Tom and Callie, and the captain from the camp.

The morning dawned clear and bright, with the sunshine playing on the snow and sparkling on the giant icicles hanging from the trees.

"Grandma would like to be buried on such a pretty day, Callie," Jurie said.

Callie, experiencing the first weeks of pregnancy, felt sick and apprehensive. She stood by the fire, shivering. She dreaded the gaping earth, the cold clods that would rattle on the coffin box.

"Poor old Granny," she said. "It's so hard to know she's gone and it just about breaks my heart. Tom and me felt sure she would come down next summer on account of th' baby. I don't know how I'm goin' to have that baby without her."

At this point, Homer called from the porch and Callie and Jurie went out to join him. Homer took Jurie's hand and they walked over to face Dr. Mayberry.

"Doc," he asked, "you mind us ridin' with you as far as th' store?"

"Why, no, Homer, but that's a long way back. Can't I get what you need, run the errand for you?"

"Me and Jurie is gettin' married, Doc. Lem Aiken over to the store is a justice."

"But, what about a license, Homer? Aren't you too young?"

"Hell, no, Doc, we ain't too young and, as for a license, it won't make no difference to Lem. He'll marry us, anyhow, and we'll get a license in the spring."

"Jurie," Homer said, "this is th' biggest and th' finest funeral ever held on th' mountain. I wish Granny could know. Look at that white coffin Doc brought. He brought a preacher, too. There must be fifty of them boys from th' camp. Look, one of 'em has a horn and he's standing in front."

When the last sounds of taps echoed in the hollow and drifted on waves to the Chimney Tops, a great silence fell upon the waiting crowd. Suddenly, a giant icicle dropped from the pine tree and stood arms out over the grave, a sparkling cross that would melt and bury itself in the earth.